a high so sweet

thornes & roses

DANI RENÉ

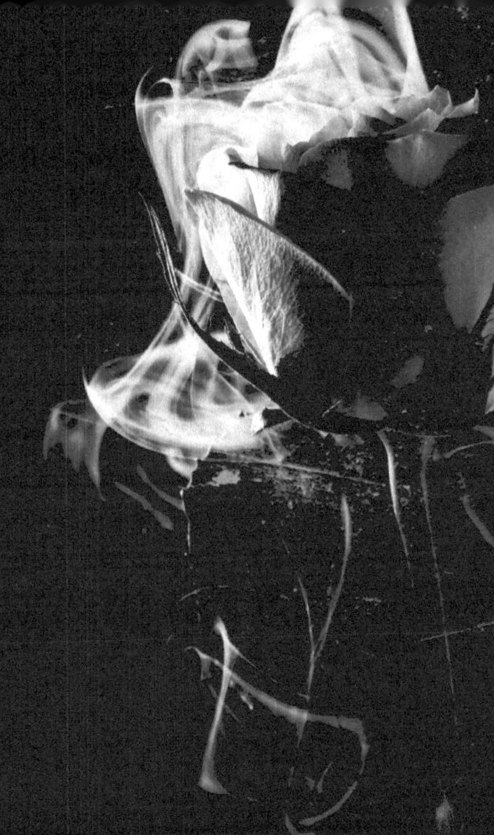

Dear Reader,

This story covers a few topics that could trigger readers. It's not a dark romance, but I do make mention of forms of abuse, especially drug use.

Please take note of this warning.

I've tried to ensure that the story shows Kalyn's strength in overcoming what she went through. In saying that, if you do decide to venture on and take this journey with Cassian and Kalyn, I hope you enjoy their emotional, and at times, steamy rollercoaster.

Mad love,
Dani, xo

We are all addicted to something that ruins us.

Quotes 'nd Notes

playlist

Run - Snow Patrol

Number - Carlie Hanson

Hard for Me - Michele Morrone

Let Her Cry - Hootie and the Blowfish

Too Much to Drink - ANTH

Fading Away - Ollie

Drinking About You - Ryan Oakes

You Broke Me First - Conor Maynard

Who Are You - SVRCINA

I Got You - Corvyx

Catch Me - Dxvn

Find the full playlist on Spotify

THORNE

dedication

To those who've been in the darkness for too long.
To those who have felt alone all their lives.
To those who are convinced they're broken.
You're strong. You're fierce. You're worthy.

prologue
Kalyn

Seventeen years old

ONE LONG SIP.

One long draw on the joint.

Two long inhales, and it feels as if my head is sparking with electric currents, bringing a smile to my face.

Inhale.

Exhale.

As the buzzing in my veins overtakes the pain and fear, I lean back against the cool concrete of the tombstone. The noise coming from the rest of the kids doesn't bother me anymore. And as the alcohol takes its hold of me, I sigh as my body tingles with the excitement of what's to come.

Tonight is my last evening in this small town, the town where everyone knows your name, and if you don't fit into their world, you're shunned. There's only one thing that I will miss about Thorne Haven, and that's *him*. But he's not here tonight. I know the Thorne brothers are off doing their own thing with their friends, and that's okay.

Actually, it's not okay.

I pull out my cell phone and unlock it. There are no messages from him. Not even a text to say goodbye. Scrolling through our chat, I ignore the sweet things he said, instead focusing on the fact that he hasn't responded to my last message.

The one where I told him I'm leaving.

There's nothing here for me—that's what my parents said. Mom wants to move to LA, where she's convinced that I'll have more opportunities than this town can offer. Dad's company was more than willing to provide him with a transfer to Hollywood Hills. And me, I have no choice but to walk away from everything I've known: school, a home I've come to love, and *him*.

"Hey, stop crying over that asshole," one of the girls from my class, Brittany, says. She's one of the popular girls, a cheerleader with big blue eyes and long blonde hair. She doesn't always talk to me, but when she does, I can't help but feel noticed.

I'm the loner in our class. And I'm happy with it that way. An emotionally distraught young woman with issues, at least that's what the psychiatrist told my folks. With each kid I know going to see a shrink, I'm not all that different, but sometimes, I feel so out of my comfort zone when it comes to these parties that I may as well be from another planet.

"I'm not crying," I tell her, tipping my chin in defiance. I take a long drag on my joint before flicking the butt and killing it with the heel of my Docs.

Music blares from a car that pulls up, shining lights over us. A few of the girls standing around shriek before they fall into a fit of giggles when they realize it's the football team. Creed Haven saunters up to Brittany, pulling her into his arms and stealing her lips with his. The guy is an asshole, but he's hot. I guess in a way that makes him think he has every right to take what he wants.

"What's up?" he greets me with a tip of his head, his eyes locking on me for a moment too long, and all I can do is shrug in response. I know he's friends with Cassian, but I don't ask the question that's burning the tip of my tongue.

I push to my feet, holding onto the tombstone as I do because my head is spinning. I didn't drink that much tonight. I'm sure of it. Glancing at the bottle I left on the ground, I realize it's empty.

Shit.

"Are you okay?" Brittany asks, concern clear in her tone, making me giggle.

"Yeah," I assure her before turning to walk off. But the moment I do, I slam into a body that's solid steel. My gaze is slightly blurry, but there's no doubt about who I've just walked into. At twenty, there's no way you can call Cassian Thorne a boy any longer—he's a man, and it shows.

"What are you doing?" he questions, his voice low, drenched in warning and disappointment, feathering in my ear when he speaks. "I thought I told you not to hang out here when I'm not around." Even though he's never touched me, kissed me, or made a move to show me he wants me, he's always been there—watching over me like a protector.

"I'm doing what every other kid here is doing," I bite back, anger surging through me when I look up into those familiar teal-color irises, and for a moment, it's as if he's spinning in front of me, but I keep my focus on his face. The anger dancing in those sparkling eyes is nothing short of fury.

"Get the fuck in my car," Cassian growls, his hand gripping my arm as he pulls me toward the black Maserati sitting amongst the trees. I stumble over the uneven ground, almost falling against his strong, muscled back. The graveyard we tend to loiter in has a forest of beautiful oak trees. And amongst them are pathways and tarred roads that people use to drive up when visiting their loved ones buried here.

"Let me go," I grit through clenched teeth as I attempt to pull free from his hold, but I know it's no use. I'm not strong enough to fight Cassian.

"Hey man," Creed's voice echoes from where we've just left him and Brittany, which causes Cass to pause. "Don't do anything I would." He chuckles, and I notice how Cassian rolls his eyes at his friend. Just as we reach his car, a couple of guys walk up the road, and I recognize Finn, Cassian's youngest brother, along with another guy I know is Creed's brother, Brody.

"You leaving already, Cass?" Finn asks his brother, a salacious smirk curling his lips as his glance flicks between us, then lands on where Cassian's grip on my arm never wavers.

"Yeah," Cass responds but doesn't offer any more information. He pulls open the passenger door and practically throws me into the leather seat.

"What's going on? You really have it hard for this kid." Finn chuckles, but Cassian's serious expression has the laugh disappearing from his brother's face.

"I'm taking her home, and then, I'll be back." He doesn't realize I can hear him through the window, or maybe he does, but he makes no move to hide the fact that he's pissed.

By the time he joins me in the car, I'm exhausted from the alcohol and the weed. The anger at my parents has eased.

He doesn't understand why I get high, why I drink. But I chose my path; I found a way to forget, to ease the burden.

"I don't like when you do shit like this," Cassian speaks as he starts the engine and glances over at me. "You need to be careful, Kaly; there are bad people out there."

I laugh.

I can't help it.

He sounds so much like my father right now, even though he's nowhere near Dad's age. "You don't have to worry about me anymore, Cassian, we're leaving tomorrow." I can't stop the bitterness from lacing my words, and I can't bring myself to look at him; instead, I focus on the window as he pulls out of the cemetery and takes the turn back into town.

We ride in silence for a while before he speaks again, "I care about you."

"Yeah?" I glance at him, taking in his profile. Sharp nose, angular jawbone, his hair is buzzed short, and his eyes, those fucking eyes that always seem to turn me into a mindless girl. He's every girl's fantasy and every guy's hero. They want to be him. They all want to be a Thorne. But nobody comes close.

"You shouldn't look at me like that," he says, but he doesn't glance my way, and I want nothing more than to climb into his lap and force him to make eye contact with me. To tell me why he doesn't want me.

"Why?" Curiosity is clear in my tone.

The corner of his mouth kicks up into an almost smile. That's one thing about Cassian Thorne; he doesn't usually show emotion. But with me, it's there in those eyes. He may be angry, happy, or even turned on, and most people won't know. But I do because he only gifts me with a window to his heart. And that's what assures me there is something more between us.

"Because you're too young for me."

"Is that why you haven't kissed me?" I challenge.

He doesn't answer. Instead, he pulls up to my house, and my heart sinks into my stomach. I don't want this to end. I want him to drive around forever, with me beside him. But I can't be, and neither can he.

I'm not the princess that gets saved by the handsome prince.

I'm the girl who gets taken from her home and sent to a goddamned school for girls where they can make sure I behave myself. It's all bullshit.

"Thanks for the ride," I tell him, knowing he won't give me what I want—him. Even at seventeen, I know what I need, what I crave; I'm not a child. But Cassian is a gentleman. He's never going to break.

So instead of giving in, he holds onto his restraint. Instead of having the one thing I do want, a connection with him, a physical one, I push open the door and get out of his car. I lean down before closing the door and say, "Goodbye." Then

I slam it shut, not giving him a chance to reply.

I turn for the house, opening the small pedestrian gate, and step inside. I know his car is still there. But I don't look. I don't turn back to see him leave me, and as I blink, the emotion trickles from my lashes, wetting my cheeks.

By the time I'm in my bedroom, I'm a mess. I shut myself in my bathroom and open the cabinet, taking everything out to find the little box I need. Inside, I pull out the sachet of white powder and cut two lines.

The moment I inhale, I forget.

I forget my pain.

I forget my heartbreak.

I forget Cassian.

Cassian

Five years later

A PARTY.

I've been looking forward to this night since last year. It's the only evening where you can do anything or be anyone. There are events that happen throughout Thorne Haven, the small town we live in, the town we own, but our Halloween Gala is probably the most infamous.

Each year Dad hosts, and I know the moment I tell my father we should try something different, he'll inform me that I've lost my mind. The thing about Thorne Haven is that there are rituals, customs that cannot be broken, no matter how much we want something new.

Every year, we have elaborate events because it's part of the town's history. Owned by two families, the Thornes, and the Havens, the town is built on a solid foundation that dates back to my ancestors. Most of the history is still hidden in the libraries of the Thorne and Haven mansions, respectively.

With my older brother Damien and his wife in London, Finn and I are left to pick up the slack. And my younger brother is not one who enjoys hard work. He loves to party hard, though, so as we get ready for this year's Halloween Gala, he's stepping in to help with the plans.

This year, we're going all out. Each year, we have a little game, and I'm so ready to find a girl who'll be able to take the edge off when I need it. I'm just not interested in the bullshit that comes with it. I loved once, but when she left, I was nothing more than a shell.

Shaking my head to clear the memories away, I focus on my closet. It's been a long time since I saw her. Five long fucking years, and she walked away from me that night, not even looking back.

Call me a fucked-up romantic, but I always believed if someone truly cared, they had to look back before leaving. It's a belief I stood by, but she didn't. Instead, she walked away, leaving me to pick up the pieces of the lies she spewed while heading off to a new life in Hollywood. And not once did she try to contact me to apologize, which means all those years I was there for her, I was the fool.

Since that night, I vowed to never allow anyone to make a fool of me again. No woman will ever get my heart. And no woman will ever make me love her. *Because I already gave my heart away.*

"What the fuck is this?" Finn's voice comes from behind me, and I glance over my shoulder to find him holding up a long black cape with a white mask. It looks like something out of a horror movie.

I chuckle, shaking my head. "Not a fucking clue," I tell him. "Maybe Dad's going as the Grim Reaper."

"That fucking sucks; I wanted to be Death," he says, annoyance clear in his tone. He glances away from the outfit and looks at me. "What are you going as?"

I haven't given it too much thought, so I shrug. "Not sure. Maybe I'll just play around with that skull face," I tell him. When I had a Skype call with Damien earlier, Nesrin said I should try getting that done for the party. It sounded like a good idea at the time since there's no mask to carry around, and I can just wear a black shirt and a pair of slacks. No need for anything elaborate.

"That's lame," Finn answers, breaking through my thoughts. "Did you hear who's back in town?" he questions when I step into my bedroom from the walk-in closet.

I glance at my brother, stopping all movement because

even though I'm not certain, I have a feeling I know what he's going to say. "Who?"

"The Narros." His voice is filled with caution when he says the name. It's the same name that's haunted my every fucking thought over the past five years. I wanted to find her, to tell her she had me, she was mine, but she was seventeen when she left, and I was far too fucking old for her. I didn't want to end up in jail, so I let her go.

The night in question has played on my mind time and again. If it wasn't for my father's influence in this town, I wouldn't be here. She was the one who didn't stand up for me when I needed it. Even though I spent years looking after her.

She wanted me that night, and I could have taken her, claimed her, made her mine. But then I would've paid dearly. That still didn't stop her from spreading a rumor, which was as dangerous as the belief her folks already had of me. They never did approve of me because they blamed me for her drinking and drug abuse, even though I was the one trying to keep her safe.

When they found the coke on her that day, I allowed them to think it was me. I let them believe I was the bad influence, not that their precious angel was doing that shit because she hated her life. And because of that, one night changed my whole life. When I arrived home that night, I found flashing lights and guys in uniform, and that's when

I learned who Kalyn Narro truly was—a fucking liar.

We used to spend our time talking late into the night. She immediately caught my attention back when I used to go to the school with Creed, a friend and one of the Havens, to pick up his brothers, not only because she was exquisitely beautiful, but because she had a fire that I'd not seen in many girls her age.

I was hooked.

Her mind worked in mysterious ways; she had a question for everything and anything. But then her grandmother died on her sixteenth birthday, and she broke. Something inside her shattered, and she turned to partying with the kids in her class.

"They're arriving this evening," Finn says suddenly, and I realize I didn't answer him earlier. He's watching me as if I were a bomb about to detonate. Perhaps I am. Maybe I'm going to explode.

And it will be all because of her—again.

"What?" The word tumbles from my mouth before I have time to think about what he's just voiced. "Does that mean...? Is she here?" Once again, my emotions are showing, those same fucking emotions I promised myself not to allow to invade my life.

Finn nods slowly. "But there's a rumor going around that something happened to her," he tells me; his voice is low, merely a whisper, and tension coils in my gut.

"What happened to her?"

"Not sure what's going on, I don't have the full scoop, but you can be sure the moment I do, you'll be the first to know," he tells me, his focus holding mine. Then he continues, "Maybe the Hollywood Hills wasn't the best choice for someone like her."

"What the fuck does that mean?" My jaw clenches so hard, I can hear my teeth grinding as I attempt to keep calm.

He shrugs slowly, his head shaking side to side as if he's about to tell me she's dead. But then he finally whispers, "she's... I think perhaps you should wait and see."

When my hands fist, he's on his feet, grabbing me around the middle with my arms locked against me. "Let me go," I growl, but it's no use. Finn knows the rage I've felt when I got back to the party that night. He saw the emotion I allowed to free itself from my usually stoic expression.

"She's here, and you're not going to lose your shit," he tells me, keeping his tone calm, but it does nothing to satiate my need for violence. I'm usually the calm one of the three Thorne brothers, but with her, I'm volatile.

"Then tell me what the fuck is wrong with her," I bite out as anger surges through me. I could take Finn down, and he knows it too, but fighting with my brother isn't going to solve anything.

"Cassian," my father's voice comes from the hallway outside my bedroom, and I shrug Finn off before stepping toward the door, just as Dad walks in. "I need you to fly out to help Damien with a meeting. But I'll have the plane ready for you to get back here for the party."

"Why can't Finn—"

"I need you out there because it's a finance issue," he interrupts me. "Please." My father isn't a man who usually asks for help; most times, he'd end up on the flight to sort out whatever shit was going on.

"Sure, yeah," I tell him with a nod. "I'll pack."

"You'll only be gone for a few days. The party is on Saturday, and I need you back." He offers me a grin before adding, "Finn will help with the arrangements while you're away. We have guests coming who haven't been to a party here before, so I'd like to impress them." He doesn't need to tell me who they are because I can only assume it's the Narros.

"Sure."

With my agreement, he turns and leaves, and I'm left wondering just how I'm going to deal with seeing her again. It's been too long, and she's no longer a child. She's all grown up, and for a moment, I consider my revenge.

1 Kalyn

The Past

S ATURDAY NIGHTS ARE MEANT FOR PARTIES.

I pull on the skinny jeans that look like they're painted on my body before I shrug on the tight-fitting top that hugs my curves and my developing breasts. I love my figure, and I hope that Cassian will finally see me as a woman.

We've been friends for a year now, and since it's my birthday, I want him to realize I'm not some teenager with a crush. There's more to me, and I can be the partner he needs.

We challenge each other.

We laugh and have fun together.

And we also find solace when we just sit and look out at the lake in silence.

I've never once felt like this about someone. Most of the guys have stayed away from me because I hang out with the Thorne brothers. They're not intimidated so much by Damien who's the eldest, but Cassian and Finn. The Thornes instill respect in this town, but the Havens enjoy introducing fear because their families rule the town. Whispers about what they do to people who cross them have floated about the hallways for years.

Mr. Thorne, their father, runs a multi-million-dollar industry, and he's known to be ruthless when it comes to business. But I've seen him with his sons, and he's nothing but a good dad.

Both families are seen as royalty in a strange, demented way. People obey them because they know if they ever cross a Thorne or a Haven, there'll be hell to pay.

The two families founded this town. Great grandfathers of both families founded Thorne Haven and settled here with their families. Even though the boys leave from time to time, they always return.

I guess, in some strange way, that does make them royalty.

I slip on my boots and lace them up. Once I'm ready, I take a quick glance in the mirror and note my barely-there makeup and glossy lips. My hair is a mass of curls, which I know Cassian likes. He's commented on it many times in the past. My stomach flip-flops when my phone buzzes and I pick it up to find his name staring back at me.

He's outside.

Grabbing my keys, I race down the stairs and out the door. Thankfully my folks are out for the evening, so I'm not questioned when I make my way to the door. As much as I love them, and I know they love me, at times, it's stifling. I do what every other kid in this town does—party hard. It's not like I'm any different.

When I get to Cassian's car, I slip into the back seat and greet the boys because Finn is in the front passenger.

"Hey, Kaly," Finn says, fist-bumping me. He's always been like a brother, teasing and taunting me at times, but also being supportive when I needed a friend. Both brothers are always there for me, but it's Cassian that's garnered more than just my friendship.

Being an only child is lonely, but the Thornes make me feel wanted, as if I'm one of them.

"What's up, sassy pants?" Cass asks, glancing at me in the rear-view mirror. It's my nickname that has me giggling. He loves to call me that because he says I spend my life sassing him instead of listening to his advice.

"Ready to party," I tell him. His dark brow arches at me, but I ignore it. He knows when I say party, it means I'll be seeking out something a little stronger than alcohol.

And even though he disagrees with it, he never stops me.

He's not my dad, just a friend. Each time I do something stupid, I expect him to leave, like everyone else does. But Cassian never walks away.

But even though I want to be strong, I want to stop turning to drugs for release, memories haunt me, and I'm left with darkness swirling in my mind. The only time they ever fizzle out is when I reach for a joint and inhale the toxic fumes.

As much as I love Cassian, I weaken when I think about being numb, being empty enough to survive the heartache. And that's when I see the disappointment in his eyes, each time I reach for a fix. Deep down, I crave the detachment that a high will bring. At least, that's what I tell myself. It's a way of escaping. A way for me not to feel the loneliness, the pain, and the heartbreak of real life.

Cassian doesn't understand that; I doubt he ever will.

As we make our way to the thickly forested area close to where the town's graveyard sits, just behind high metal fences, the sound system blares around me, surrounding me with Corvyx's voice singing "I Got You." As I listen to the lyrics and glance at Cassian, I wonder if the emotions in the words of the song will ever be something he feels about me.

Shaking my head of the wayward thought, I focus on the drive. When Cassian pulls up to the parking spot and kills the engine, he's out of the car and rounding the back to open my door. It's something he's always done. I step out, and he doesn't move out of the way, which has his body looming over mine.

He reaches for a lock of my hair and tugs it gently. "Happy birthday, sweet girl," he coos, and my body goes into overdrive. My stomach tumbles, my heart leaps into my throat, and for a moment, I pray he's going to kiss me. I pray with everything in me that those perfect lips will touch mine. "Behave yourself tonight, or there will be consequences."

His threat does not alleviate the heat coursing through my veins. And my thighs squeeze together at his nearness and the fact that his lips are inches from mine.

"Like what?" I sass him. In an attempt to fold my arms across my chest, my hands brush against him, which has him stepping back as if I've broken the spell he was under.

"Don't you worry," he tells me quickly. "Just behave." The warning is clear—don't do drugs. But then he takes my hand and tugs me deeper into the woods, where the rest of the student body is already partying.

That was the closest we've come to kissing. To touching. Yeah, we've held hands before, but this is different. Something has shifted, but I can't quite put my finger on it. I'm almost certain his feelings are reciprocated, but he has never verbally admitted it.

We stop at the truck that's filled with two kegs, and Cassian grabs two Solo cups. He fills them both and hands me one.

"The most you're having," he warns.

"It's my birthday." I'm sure I sound like a whiny kid, but it really is my birthday, and if he expects me to sip on one beer all night, he has another thing coming.

We move toward the music, which is blaring from one of the cars. I spot the Haven brothers—Creed, Keirin, and Brody—as we make our way to where they're huddled with a few girls.

"Cass, my man," Creed greets, and the guys give a one-shoulder hug. Creed's deep green eyes land on me, and even in the dim light, there's a fire burning in them. "Pretty girl. Want to come play with a Haven?"

"Okay, enough," Cassian admonishes his friend who only chuckles, but his gaze still drinks me in. The other two Haven brothers laugh, their eyes flicking between Cass and Creed. Usually, they follow Creed around as if he were their leader. He's the eldest of the three which, I can only assume, makes him alpha, as if they're a wolf pack.

As the night wears on. I find another drink, and another. I'm leaning against a tree trunk when a couple of seniors from school come over to me, one on each side. One of them leans in to whisper in my ear, "Want to party with us?" His voice is low, filled with desire, and even though I know I shouldn't, I nod.

Cassian hasn't come to find me. He's with Creed and

Finn, and right now, I'm lonely. I follow the guys to a car, where they slip into the back seat, dragging me in along with them.

It doesn't take long for the white powder to make its appearance. And seconds later, I'm inhaling deeply. The numbness that's so welcome takes over, and I lean back against the seat.

My eyes are closed, the high slowly taking me to the clouds, when I feel a hand on my arm, trailing over my hypersensitive skin. Tingles erupt along with goosebumps, and I can't stop a smile from playing on my lips. I needed to forget tonight. I craved the numbing sensation, and as it holds me hostage, I enjoy it.

Another hand grips my thigh, squeezing ever so slightly before trailing its way up. Before I can react, fingers brush between my legs, but I push them away.

"No. I'm not into that," I mumble, but I don't know if they heard me. My voice sounds far away. Everything seems to start spinning, and all I feel are fingers and hands. "Please, stop it."

"Aww, come on, birthday girl. Let's party," a deep voice whispers in my ear. His hand grips my breast harshly, causing me to cry out in pain, and suddenly, it's gone, and cold air hits me. I'm slung over someone's shoulder, and being upside down doesn't help the spinning.

"Put me down," I beg, attempting to punch whoever it is

in the back, but they ignore me. With every step, I'm sent spiraling, and when I'm finally righted, my feet firmly on the ground, I glance up into furious teal eyes.

"What the fuck are you playing at?" Cassian's voice is rough as rage takes hold of him. Fire blazes in his eyes, and for the first time in my life, I'm afraid of him.

"I—I was..." I glance over my shoulder, and that's when I see Creed and Finn punching the fuck out of two guys. "Was that...?"

"They almost fucking assaulted you, and you wouldn't have even known." Cassian's words are like ice to my veins, my high almost dissipating, but I wish it were that easy to get rid of. Dizziness hits me hard, and I fall into Cassian's arms. "Fucking hell," he curses, helping me into his car and shutting the door behind me.

When he slips into the driver's side, he looks over at me. I must be a mess. Tears burn my eyes, and when I blink, they slip free, trickling down my cheeks. This is why he doesn't want me. I'm too much work.

I don't blame him.

I can't.

Why would a good guy like him want a fuck-up like me? I spend my life making a mess of everything around me. And this time, it's no different. I wanted to celebrate my birthday, but I ended up in a situation where I could've been hurt.

"I'm taking you home," Cassian tells me before handing me a bottle of chilled water. My knight in shining armor is a boy I'll never have.

Happy ever after isn't something I can ever have. Not with Cassian. I'm far too destructive. The realization hits me in the chest, and a sob bubbles up, escaping my lips before I have time to push it back down.

"I'm sorry," I whisper, not looking at the man beside me. He may only be eighteen, but he's more mature than I'll ever be.

I'm sure I won't ever have a chance with him.

And that's when my heart shatters even more.

Kalyn

The Present

THE CAR DOESN'T SLOW DOWN AS WE MAKE OUR WAY through the town that borders Thorne Haven. With every mile that passes and the closer I get to my childhood home, my shoulders tense, my stomach twists, and my chest tightens.

I never thought I'd ever see the sleepy town again, but as we head back to my past, the nervous energy in my gut makes me feel queasy. I'm almost certain he's no longer in town. He must've left years ago because if there's one thing I know about Cassian Thorne, it's that he's not someone who can sit still. He had dreams, and there is no way he would not have followed through on those.

He's always had wanderlust, and I'm sure with his family's money, he is able to travel and live anywhere in the world. All I can do is pray he's taken the opportunity and moved far away from this sleepy little pocket of beauty he once called home.

The town car finally comes to a crawl as we head up the hill, which will take us to my childhood home, but not before passing Thorne manor. The enormous mansion stands proudly amongst the trees, the rooftops just visible in between the greenery.

Yellow and gold leaves color the sidewalk, as the trees that line either side of the road turn to their fall shades. It's almost Halloween, and the weather has turned chilly. There is rain in the forecast for the rest of the week, and I wonder briefly if there'll be a gala on Saturday. It's one of the most talked-about events in town, even people from out of state travel to attend the infamous Thorne Gala.

The thought sends a flurry of nerves fluttering in my stomach at the idea of Cassian coming home to attend. But even if he does, he'll be dressed up, most probably, which means it will be harder to spot him.

We pull up the long driveway that leads to the place I lost my heart, mind, and soul, and for a moment, I'm sure it's changed. It doesn't look as big or as haunting as it used to, but then again, I was seventeen, the last time I saw it. A broken teenager who escaped her pain with drugs and alcohol.

"So, this is your home?" the voice from beside me startles me because my mind had wandered to another place. Another time. But I can't focus on the past, so I glance at the man beside me.

I nod slowly. "It was," I respond honestly; the raspy tone of my voice is the only clue that emotion has taken hold of me.

"Hey," he says as he scoots closer to me, taking my hand in his. "This is for the best." He presses a kiss to my knuckles, and I don't miss how he glances at the ring on my finger, the princess cut diamond he slid onto my hand only a week ago. When I said yes, I didn't think the guilt would eat away at me, and now, as we pull up to the one place I never wanted to return to, I realize there's no more hiding away. I have to face my mistakes, my past, and the one man who still holds my heart.

The reason we're here is not to reminisce on days gone by but to say a final goodbye. I just wish my father was here. Even though he couldn't make the trip due to his illness, I still miss my dad being close.

I think about the last time I saw him, two days ago, when I told him we needed to get this done. He looked so much older, frailer, with his hair graying and the illness taking hold of him like I never thought possible. Even though they caught it early, the treatments have stolen his energy. All I can do is pray that he overcomes it, that it doesn't spread into his stomach and liver, but there are no guarantees in life.

My chest tightens at the thought, reminding myself of what I've already lost, *who* I've lost. Tears burn my eyes as I push open the door and step out of the town car. My gaze taking in the three-story mansion, I notice how ancient it looks from out here. Since living in Los Angeles, where everything is glass and steel, I breathe a sigh of relief, taking in the darkness of the wooden beams and black metal terraces. Most of Thorne Haven is old, with antiques and open brick.

"Are you okay, sweetheart?" Paulo, my fiancé, questions in a whisper, his arm wrapping around my shoulders. It's meant to come from a place of love and affection, but I know it's more intrusive to find out if I'm feeling like snorting white powder up my nose.

"I'm fine," I tell him before stepping onto the porch and over the threshold as our driver pushes open the door. My heels clink against the tiles as I step inside the home I came to love. I'm different now, yet still the same. I'm older, more mature, but the lie I told still haunts me. The addiction I allowed to eat away at me is still there, lurking beneath the bright, fake smiles and designer clothes.

It's all smoke screens.

I take in the entrance. Nothing has changed. It's as if the house was stuck in a frozen state with us not living in it. Compared to most homes in Thorne Haven, ours is modest.

"Are you sure?" Paulo asks as he sidles up beside me, causing me to glance up at him. He's the man I agreed to marry. The same man who's been my co-star for the past two years, and the same one who's now found his way into my home.

I wasn't ready to bring him to Thorne Haven, but Dad insisted. For some reason, he likes Paulo. Perhaps it's because Paulo was there for me when I went to *rehab* the first time, and the second. If only Dad knew the truth.

Maybe it's because he thinks that Paulo can save me. What he doesn't know is that my fiancé is the one who's feeding my habit, one party at a time. But if I were to admit it, I know Dad wouldn't believe me.

I nod my head because I realize I haven't answered him, and he doesn't like being ignored. The thoughts of my father have my chest tightening. I can't look at the disappointment in my father's gaze anymore. I've spent the past few months watching him get sick, get weak, knowing I've fucked up. More so than usual.

Paulo has seen to it we're in his debt. I don't know how long I can survive this, but for my father to get his treatment, I play the game until I can find a way out of this shitshow my life has become.

"Yes." I smile up at the man who says he loves me. "I'm going to shower," I tell him, ignoring the glare he pins me with. The heat of his stare is nothing short of scorching, as if he's trying to burn me alive. I know he'll ensure I'm pliant this evening. And every night after. I'll spend my life with him in a blur of highs, and a series of lows.

"I'll be up in a bit to check on you," Paulo says, his voice tinged with fake concern, and I have to fight the urge to roll my eyes. "Kalyn." My name is a warning on his tongue, so I nod, but I don't lock my eyes on his. "While we're here, don't forget where you belong."

For a long moment, I stay silent, tears burning my eyes.

"Are you listening to me, Kalyn?" His voice is terse with frustration. "Because if you don't, you know I have something to ensure you obey." The threat is there, reminding me what I've gotten myself into. His steps behind me send a shudder through me, and when his hand grips my arm, his fingers dig into the flesh, causing me to wince. Then Paulo leans in, "And you know how much I like when you submit to me."

I swallow the lump in my throat and nod. "Yes, Paulo."

"Good girl," he coos the two words that used to make me feel appreciated, now they leave fear in my gut. "I don't like repeating myself." He releases me, and I finally allow myself to breathe. When I walk, he doesn't follow, but I know it won't be long before he's ensuring I'm malleable.

In my bedroom, I shut the door and lean against the wooden surface, breathing deeply. I want nothing more than to run into the forest and get lost in the darkness, but I can't leave the house right now. Not when I have Paulo watching me like a hawk, and I know he'll be coming up here to make sure I don't overdose.

A shiver wracks through me when I step deeper into the room and find nothing has changed. When I left five years ago, I cried all the way to the airport, and when we landed on the West Coast, I knew I should have done things differently.

With my parents.

With my schooling.

With Cassian.

Guilt has eaten at me for years, and even though I haven't seen him yet, the dread I feel for what I did that night hasn't left me. My father believed me, so did my mother, and when I realized what I'd said, it was too late.

In my bathroom, I turn on the shower and strip off my clothes. The hot spray stings as it hits my skin, but I don't turn on the cold tap; I need to feel the pain to remind myself why I'm here. A quick glance at my toiletry bag that I set on the counter has me moving without a second thought, and I find what I'm looking for as the room fills with steam.

I'm nothing more than a blur in the mirror, and I inhale deeply, sniffing back the powder that's kept me sane for most of my life. I tip my head back and close my eyes.

I didn't choose to do this. It happened one night when I was vulnerable. When I lost the one woman who loved me unconditionally, I broke. Alcohol and drugs were easy to get when you had the money and grew up in a town where every kid had problems. I hid it well for a long while.

Until *that* night.

Until the moment I fell over the edge and hurt Cassian.

And the moment I lay my gaze on him again, I know forgiveness will not be something he'll ever offer me. I wouldn't ask it of him, but I know if he's still around and I do see him again, all I can do is apologize for the mistake I made.

"Tell us where you've been, young lady?" Dad grits angrily. His fists clench, and I am almost certain he can smell the alcohol wafting from me. I shouldn't have done what I did, but I couldn't help it. It's a poor excuse. Even I know that.

"Was it that boy that hangs out with you?" This comes from Mom, her concern clear. I glance down, noticing my clothes are torn. I wanted to avoid them, so I tried climbing the trellis that leads to my bedroom. Only, I fell, ripping my top.

It looks bad.

It looks...

"Kalyn Narro," Dad utters with rage dripping on every syllable. "Are you drunk? Have you been taking drugs? I told you that Thorne boy was bad news, but you don't listen to me." His voice is loud, booming through the

room, all the while making my head spin. "Tell me, young lady! Are you on drugs? Who gave them to you? Is that Thorne boy you're hanging around with dealing drugs?"

Anger surges at his questions. I wish Cassian had touched me. I wish he had kissed me. Something. Anything. All I wanted was some indication I wasn't being a stupid little girl, but he didn't.

"Kalyn, is that Thorne boy giving you drugs?"

"Talk to us, Kalyn?"

"What happened?"

Too many questions are fired at me. Images dance in my mind. Cassian. His car. His goodbye. Even his words of encouragement didn't hit home like they usually do. Not tonight.

"Kalyn, did he force you to take something?"

"I..."

Dad storms forward, gripping my arms and shaking me as if I were a rag doll. My head spins due to the alcohol and weed, and everything turns blurry. I want to go to my room, but the hold Dad has on my arms is like a vise, and I know I'm not going to escape anytime soon.

Not until I give him an answer.

"Tell me!" His demand rings in my ears. And I can't find words. I'm not sure how to free myself from this interrogation. It's all too much, and my eyes burn with tears. I need to get away, to hide. "Is it the Thorne boy who did this to you?"

"Yes! Okay!" I hiss angrily, agreeing to something. I can't remember what, but I give my father what he wants. "It's him. It's always been him, and it won't ever be anyone else." Tears track their way down my cheeks as my heart *cracks at the thought of leaving Thorne Haven and not seeing Cassian every day.*

"Are you happy now? Leave me alone; you've already ruined my life." I push away from my father and race to my bedroom, shutting myself inside. I lock the door so they can't come in; I need to be alone. I rush to the bathroom and turn on the taps of my shower.

By the time I'm under the spray, my mind clears of the fog. And as the realization of what I've just told my father hits me, a sob breaks free from my lips, and I drop to my knees under the scalding water.

I lied.

I fucked up.

And my father isn't going to let this lie.

That night was a mistake. When my father called the police, I was downstairs, begging him to stop. I told my father it was a lie. I told him I only said it to stop them from questioning me, but the deed was done, and I had no way of stopping it.

My father is headstrong, and when he gets an idea in his head, he doesn't let up. Thankfully, I was able to talk to Cassian's father when he got to our home to sort the incident out. But Cassian wasn't there. He didn't come with his dad, and I didn't blame him. I wouldn't want to look at me either.

Thankfully, the charge was dropped when I finally confessed it was a lie, but the damage had been done. Even though Mr. Thorne had made sure nobody spoke of it again, it was a lie I uttered, not realizing what it meant until after it fell from my lips.

The drugs course through my veins, reminding me of the euphoria that takes hold of me as it warms me from the inside out. Numbness washes over me like a wave dancing along the shore. Everything spins for a moment before it becomes clearer. I know I shouldn't be doing this again, but I can't help myself. My blood zings through me, and it feels as if I'm flying through clouds.

When I finally open my eyes, I can't see anything in the mirror because it's steamed up. Reaching for the cool glass, I swipe my hand along it, clearing the mist to take in my distorted reflection.

"I'm sorry," I whisper to the emptiness. My throat constricts when I think about saying those two words to Cassian. But it's the non-response I know I'll receive from him that makes the tears trickle from my eyes, burning their path down my cheeks.

It's time to face my fuck-ups.

It's time to see him again.

I just don't know how to apologize to the one person I hurt more than myself.

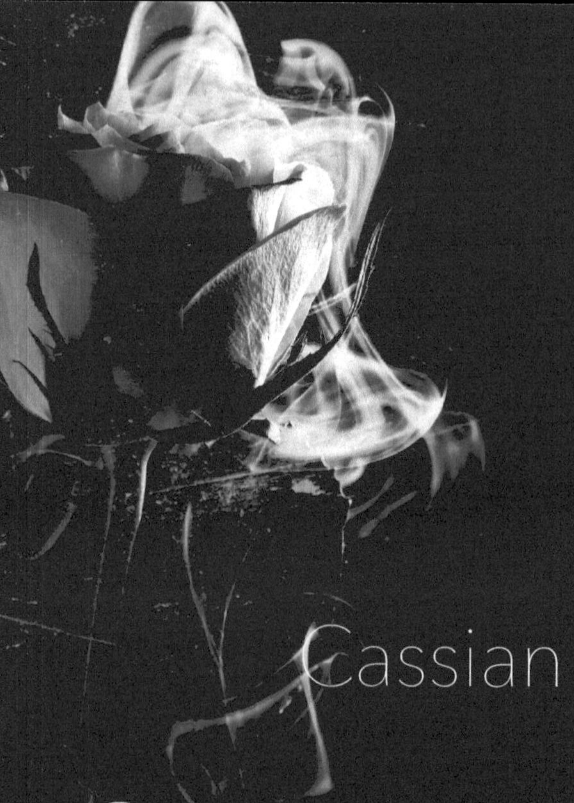

Cassian

Settling into a seat opposite my brother, Damien, I pick up the mug of coffee and take a long sip. The meeting with the board went well, and they're happy to continue our growth into Europe, which means Damien will be busier as the year progresses. It also means Finn and I will need to travel out here more often.

It's been a few months since I've seen my older brother, and I have to be honest, I miss him being in Thorne Haven. But he's needed here to run the British offices of Thorne Industries.

"What's happening back home?" he questions, his narrowed gaze locked on me as he leans back in the expensive leather chair behind his enormous desk. His blue eyes focus on me, and it's almost as if he can see the war waging within me.

"She's back. She's returning to Thorne Haven," I tell him. I don't need to explain who I'm talking about because there would only be one person who would make my voice turn dark with anger and pain.

He tips his head to the side, surprise evident on his expression as he regards me. He knows what happened that night when I tried to act like a hero. The tension in the room intensifies when he leans forward, his elbows on the desk, his hands clasped, and I notice just how white his knuckles are turning. "Are you sure?"

"Yeah." I nod. "Finn said he heard they're coming back from LA because *something* happened. I'm not sure what," I tack on because I know he'll ask for more information.

He ponders this for a while. "Do you want me to ask our team to dig into it?" I did consider doing this, but if I'm completely honest with myself, I don't think it would make a difference. My anger has kept me strong for so long, I'm not sure I can live with anything else.

Shaking my head, I sigh. "No." I look at my brother as the words fall from my lips. "If she *is* back, I'll have to face her," I tell him. "And she's going to pay for what she did." I finally make my decision. At first, I thought I could run her out of Thorne Haven, it would be the easiest thing to do, but that's not what I want anymore. I need her to feel the betrayal I did. It might be childish to toy with someone, but she did it to me, and I need her to understand how painful it was to learn how a lie, one simple untruth, could change your life.

"Cass," Damien says, bringing my attention back to the present, and I can hear the wariness in his tone. Even though he's the eldest, I've always been calmer when it comes to revenge, when it comes to making sure those who fuck over a Thorne pay.

But this time, I can't stop myself from needing to see her cry.

"She was young, immature. Kalyn was dealing with demons you couldn't cure for her. She wanted a hero, but she needed professional help," Damien's voice is calm as he tries to assure me of this. I knew she was. It's the reason I didn't take our friendship to the next level. But it doesn't matter, not anymore.

"That doesn't matter," I say while meeting his cool stare. My fist clenches around the mug. "She lied. I don't like people who lie, you know this."

He nods. "I do, but perhaps there was a reason for what she did," he assures me, but it's not going to change my mind.

"I don't give a shit. I was there for her. What if Nesrin lied about you? What if she spread rumors and got away with it?" I shouldn't bring his wife into it. I love my sister-in-law, she's a wonderful woman, but I need Damien to understand what it felt like to be blindsided like I was.

"Does Creed know she's back?" he questions, ignoring my queries, and I don't blame him. My brother is like me, and I know if Nesrin did what Kaly did, he would never have forgiven her. Fuck, he would've probably sent her packing right back to the starry skies of Hollywood.

"Not sure. I haven't spoken to him in a while." I finish my coffee and relax back into the soft leather of the chair. I have to get ready for my flight home, but I'd much prefer staying in London with Damien and Nesrin than to go back to my past.

"Cass, promise me you won't do something stupid," Damien pleads with me, and as much as I'd love to appease my brother, I can't. He stares at me for a long while, but I don't answer. Damien sighs, shaking his head as he pushes to his feet. "Just be careful," he warns.

"Because you know I'm right. I should get my vengeance for the lies she spread about me," I finally find my words. "You can't expect me to ignore the fact that my life imploded."

For a long moment, he's silent, and I half-expect him to refuse. I think he's going to say I'm being an asshole, but then he does answer. "I get that. Trust me, I fucking get it, but remember, we're all grown-up now. We're adults."

I chuckle at that because as much as I know he's right, he also knows nobody fucks with a Thorne. "We may be, but that doesn't mean we can forgive and forget."

"What are you not forgiving and forgetting?" Nesrin's gentle tone comes from the doorway, and I turn to find my sister-in-law leaning against the doorjamb, her arms folded across her chest as she regards her husband and me.

"Nothing, sweet sister," I respond, going to pull her into a hug, which she allows, but I can tell she doesn't believe me. I don't blame her. Nesrin Thorne is far too intelligent to believe my bullshit.

When I step back, Nesrin pins me with a disbelieving stare before shaking her head. "Don't do stupid shit," she tells me before leaning up on her tiptoes to press a kiss to my cheek.

"I'm the levelheaded one," I inform her, but chuckle when she rolls her eyes at my insistence. "I'm serious. Have you met my brothers?" I tease with a smile, which earns me a giggle in response.

"Yeah, sure," she answers as she sidles into Damien's arms. "I can't believe you're leaving so soon. You just got here."

"I know, but Dad wants me back there for the gala." I pull my phone from my pocket when it vibrates, and I find a message from Finn. "And it seems if I don't get back, Finn will commit murder because I left him alone with our folks."

"I get that." Nesrin grins. "Tell him I say hi. You both have to visit soon. We need to have a family reunion."

"Sounds good," I agree. "I better head to the airstrip before the jet leaves without me." I shrug on my suit jacket and button it up. Knowing everything I must do before the event on Saturday, I'm thankful I'm returning a day early. I thought about staying an extra night just so I didn't have to deal with the final preparations for the gala, but the meeting went so well, Damien and I secured the contract that will see Thorne Industries netting another fifty million.

But the thought of getting home has me exhausted because it's going to be non-stop this weekend. Not only that, but I'm also about to deal with a ghost from my past. And this time, the high of seeing her won't be as sweet as I would want it to be.

When someone you love returns after a long while, it should be a happy occasion, but knowing she'll be so close, doesn't leave me with thoughts of exhilaration.

Nesrin hugs me once more, nestling her head against my chest, and for a moment, I remember the first time I met her. Her mother married our father, and that's when Damien fell hard. He didn't want to, but there was no denying the tension between them, the love and affection he experienced, was nothing short of a fucking fairy tale.

When she steps back, I take her in. A woman who's strong and independent, but still, a gentle soul who challenges my brother daily as if she was born to do it. They're a power couple, and my chest tightens when I realize something—I want what they have.

"See you soon, brother." Damien shakes my hand, pulling me in for a one-armed hug before I walk out of his office and make my way down to the waiting car. It's time to go, to see *her* again, and to finally put the demons of my past behind me.

But as I slip into the back seat, I wonder if I'll ever be able to do that.

Can I truly forgive her for the shit she put me through?

Kalyn

S ILENCE.

Opening my eyes, I stare up at the ceiling. Beside me, Paulo still sleeps. I don't look at him, but I can feel his warmth radiating toward me. I don't remember how I got to bed, but I'm certain he picked me up and carried me into the bedroom.

Last night was a mistake. The strength I thought I'd found in my mind came crashing down the moment I walked back into Thorne Haven.

I'm broken.

I'm weak.

Tears burn my eyes when I think about how broken I truly

am. And I know the moment I see Cassian again, I'll shatter once more. When I was younger, I thought I was invincible. Parties were the norm, drinking was expected, and getting high was an escape from our everyday bullshit lives.

But I made a mistake and betrayed the only person who cared for me. I'm not saying my parents weren't there, but there were expectations set for me. I needed to be mature in my decisions. They didn't raise me to be a weak person, and I know I've disappointed them both, time and again.

But with addiction comes recklessness.

I glance over at Paulo, whose long dark lashes flutter against his cheeks. He's charming, a woman's dream man—tall, dark, and handsome. But I'm not just any woman, and Paulo, he's not the man who holds my heart.

Pushing from my bed, I nudge open the curtains to take in the bright sunshine, which blinds me for a moment. The view from my bedroom overlooks the woods, the same forest where I met Cassian. Losing myself in a memory, I smile.

My heart is thudding wildly as I listen to the howling amongst the thick trunks of oak trees. Two girls from my class are ahead of me, each slinking down onto their haunches as they attempt to hide, but there is no hiding from the game.

Burnt roses were left in our lockers, which means we're the prey. It's a game the Thorne and Haven brothers came up with a long time ago, and I never thought I would be one of the chosen girls. But when I opened my locker earlier after math class, there it was, waiting for me.

A crack in the distance has the other two girls squealing, and I inhale a deep breath before running deeper into the forest. I know there's a lake that's hidden by the trees, so I make my way toward it, hoping the guys won't find me. But even as I think it, I know it's a lie.

The only boy whom I want to find me is him.

Cassian Thorne.

When I first laid eyes on him, I knew he would be the love of my life. It might sound stupid, perhaps like a teenage crush. But there's something about him, the cold, aloof, yet protective demeanor that makes my stomach tumble with excitement when he gazes at me.

Teal eyes. Sharp features and full lips only seem to make me want to stare at him. He has caught me a few times, and even then, I couldn't bring myself to look away. If humans were perfect, I'm almost certain that Cassian would be right up there with the best of them. At times, I wonder if he's even real. Call it infatuation, I don't care, because he has shown me he's good. Deep down inside.

By the time I reach the lake, I'm out of breath, my legs ache, and my chest is tight with exertion. Stopping for a moment, I lean against the rough bark of the tree trunk and catch my breath.

It's silent.

My ears prick when I hear rustling, but it doesn't seem to be too close, so I don't panic. But as I calm my erratic breaths, a hand suddenly covers my mouth, and I scream into the soft yet strong palm covering my lips that muffles the sound of my shock.

"Caught you, pretty girl," the deep, familiar voice of the one boy I wanted to touch me feathers along my ear, and a shiver of nervous energy shoots through me.

I nod slowly, hoping he'll release me. For a moment, he doesn't move, and then his hand falls, and he rounds me, stopping right in front of me. Even in the darkness, those teal eyes steal my attention.

The corner of his mouth kicks up into a dark, dangerous smirk. "Seems like you're coming with me to prom," he tells me. That's the rule. Since he's a senior, he can ask me to any dance throughout the school year. And at his question, my heart thunders in my ear. "Unless you'd like to go with one of my brothers?"

"No!" The word comes out quickly, breathlessly. "I mean, yes, I'd like to go with you." I finally respond in a whisper, and he grins, which only seems to make him handsomer than I ever imagined.

"Good," he says, seeming to be happy with my answer as he slips his hand in mine. "I think we'll have fun."

"Darling," Paulo's voice rings out from behind me, dragging me from a happier time to my current heartache. "Come back to bed," he coaxes, but I can't face him.

"I need to freshen up," I respond, focusing on the carpet instead of him. "We have to go shopping for the party tomorrow night." Even as I say it, my stomach twists with anxiety because the moment I walk into the Thorne mansion, my life will change.

"You know," he starts, keeping his voice low, filled with danger, and I know what's coming—a threat, "Last night, I could've told them." It's a warning. His intimidation has always worked because Paulo knows I don't want my family to learn about my transgressions. He has all the power here, and I have nothing but my need to forget.

"I know." I don't turn to look at him. I can't. If I do, I'll break down, I'll show emotion, and it will only confirm just how much he can break me if he opens his mouth. The truth will send my family into disarray, and I have no one to blame but myself. My father is ill, and I cannot bear the thought of my mistakes hurting him. I've done enough to hurt those I love.

"Then join me in bed," he whispers; this time, it's a gentle murmur. It's always the same. If I try to show strength in the face of his commands, he doesn't like it. He prefers me to be a docile kitten, obeying every whim he has.

With tears pricking my eyes, I turn toward the bed and return to the sheets where the devil himself waits for me. And as I slip under the covers, into his arms, I shut my eyes and picture the teal eyes that have always given me solace.

It's no use in holding out hope that he's thought of me. There isn't any reason for me to believe he even remembers the girl who almost tarnished his name. But then again, Cassian was never one to forget things, and I wasn't just a girl to him; I know that.

He cared.

Which means he'll only hate me more than he did before.

And when he sees me again, I shudder to think what he's going to do.

As Paulo's hands roam my frame, I picture the anger in Cassian's eyes, I imagine the fury in his words. And as my fiancé's fingers tease me, I find pleasure in the fact that I want it to be another man's hands on me, hurting me, making me pay the price for what I did.

I crave the pain.

I hunger for the punishment.

And I know there is only one person to offer me solace.

Cassian

BY THE TIME I ARRIVE BACK, I'M EXHAUSTED BECAUSE I spent the flight doing my research. When Kalyn walked out of Thorne Haven with lies on her tongue and deceit in her words, I closed my heart and mind to her.

To me, she didn't exist anymore.

Even as I think it, I know it's a lie.

Stalking through the hallway toward my room, I focus on getting a shower before having to deal with my father and his wife, Nesrin's mother. The moment I step over the threshold of my bedroom, though, I find my brother on the bed, his back leaning against the headboard, lounging with his feet crossed at the ankle as if he owns the space.

"What are you doing in here?" I ask before shoving the suitcase onto the opposite side of the bed from Finn.

His eyes, dark brown like our mother's, follow me, but he doesn't say a word. His focus is on me as I move to the closet while unbuttoning my shirt. But when I head back into the bedroom, I find he hasn't moved.

"What the fuck is going on?" My voice is tight with tension. I'm tired, I don't need Finn's games, and if there's one thing my brother enjoys, it's his games.

"There's something you should know," he finally speaks when I don't move, pinning him with a frustrated glare. When I don't answer, he continues, "I've overheard a few things you should be made aware of before tomorrow night." But the more he draws this out, the more frustrated I become.

"If you don't tell me what the fuck—"

"Kalyn is engaged," he breathes, his voice low, but I hear him. "She's here with her folks and the fiancé."

"I know."

Finn's mouth pops open in shock, his eyes wide as he regards me, then a sly grin curls his lips. "You and Damien were doing some digging," he says.

"No. I actually did some digging on my own on the way home. The flight was long, and I needed a distraction," I inform him before shrugging off my shirt and throwing it in the hamper near the door. "I wanted to be ready for whatever hits me when I get back and found some articles about her engagement."

I stop all movement, locking my gaze on my brother's. He doesn't seem too perturbed by my admission, but Finn knows me, and he must have known I would have done my own research on the girl who nearly broke me.

He sits up, rubbing his hands together. "So, what are we going to do about it?" He arches a brow at me, a smile on his face that tells me he's willing to do this with me. I would've gotten my revenge alone with no qualms, but with Finn by my side, I know we'll be able to send her back to Hollywood.

"She doesn't belong in Thorne Haven, not anymore," I tell Finn. "I have a feeling we may need the Havens for this." I don't want to include Creed Haven in this; the asshole has no morals. But if I need something done and want to keep my hands clean, he's the one I'd call on. He loves blood, would happily get his hands dirty. And when it comes to torture, Creed enjoys listening to the screams of those he needs information from.

"Well, I'm ready for anything." Finn grins before pushing to his feet. "Oh, by the way, your mattress is fucked," he remarks while walking by me.

"Jesus, did you have a woman in my bed while I was gone?" I bite out through clenched teeth, frustration coursing through my veins at my youngest brother.

He doesn't respond, but the chuckle that vibrates through

his chest is my answer. *Asshole.* My brother is one of the most frustrating guys I've ever come across, but there's one thing about him, he's loyal to a fault, and when you cross him, I'd feel sorry for you.

Being the youngest, he's always struggled with being *seen* by our father. Dad has always favored Damien over us, which I didn't complain about because I wanted more than carrying on a legacy. But for Finn, he *wanted* to work at Thorne Industries while my need was to travel.

After that night, Dad laid down the law and forced me to focus on school and getting my business degree so I could step into my position at Thorne Industries. My hands fist at my sides when I recall everything that went down. How my best friends were there for me when *she* wasn't.

Shaking my head to clear it, I focus on the need for a shower and strip before heading to my en-suite. Turning on the cold taps, I step in and hiss at the icy spray.

She's engaged.

She belongs to someone else.

But it's all a lie. I know it is because she'll always belong to me.

"I'm so... I don't know," Kalyn murmurs as she draws circles in the sand. We've come to the lake, hidden amongst the trees, to talk about Kalyn's sadness. The moment I saw her at school today, I knew something was off. Even though I'm a senior and shouldn't

be spending time with a sixteen-year-old girl, I can't leave her.

The pull toward Kalyn Narro has been innate for me. I haven't had a choice in how I feel about her, and it seems this is one time I'm right because she wants me too.

Even though I haven't done anything with her, other than talk, flirt a bit, there is still some strange agony that tugs at my chest when I take her home, when I say goodbye to her, because I'm convinced each time I do, it will be forever.

And that scares the shit out of me.

"Broken? Tortured?" I offer, because that's what she looks like with her dark lashes and eyeliner. When she glances at me with those hazel eyes, I find myself lost in them. Even with tears shimmering on her long lashes, there's something alluring about her, pulling me into her orbit and not allowing me to leave.

"Yeah," she finally whispers. "Both of those. And a million more." She turns her focus to the ground, the stick she's holding swirling in the almost black mud that's underfoot. "How can life fuck you so hard?"

A laugh tumbles from my lips at her honest question. She's not wrong there. Even though I'm privileged, I have a great dad, amazing brothers who I'm close to, life does fuck you, and at times, it doesn't even ask for permission.

"I don't know," I finally answer when I notice she's waiting on an answer. Those wide eyes lock on mine, holding me hostage, and I'm drawn to her like a moth to a flame. And I know if I get any closer, I'll only burn. "Maybe we should get back before your folks send out

a search party.”

Unlike the other parents in Thorne Haven, Kalyn's care about her. They love her deeply, and they would do anything for her. It's clear. She's lucky to have that, and I wonder if she even realizes it.

"A search party?" she teases, a smile gracing her pretty face, and it takes everything inside me not to lean in and kiss her, to steal her lips with mine and show her just how good it feels to let go.

"You know they treat you like a fragile doll," I taunt, "but that's not what you are. Is it, Kaly?"

Her eyes sparkle with amusement, and she shakes her head slowly. "Maybe not. But I get it; I'm young." There's sadness in her tone, and I wonder if that's because she feels immature around me or if she wants to enjoy her life and be an adult. I should tell her it's not all it's hyped up to be, but I don't.

Instead, I watch her for a long moment.

A pretty little star.

"Let's go," I say, pushing to my feet before I offer her a hand, which she stares at for a long moment before accepting. I pull her to stand, and she stumbles into me. I'm not sure if it's because I pulled her too quickly, hoping for her to plaster herself against me, or if it's her doing. Either way, I know that this girl, this shining star, will always be mine.

When I finally turn off the taps, the water is like ice against me. That was the first night I wanted to claim her, and it wasn't the last. And even now, against my better judgment, knowing what I know, I want nothing more than to steal her away from that bullshit fiancé she has and show her just how much she belongs to me—a Thorne.

Kalyn

IT'S ALMOST TIME FOR THE PARTY, AND I'M NOT SURE I want to go. The infamous gala at the Thorne mansion. I've heard whispers that there are only two brothers in town, and I'm guessing it would be Cassian and Finn. Damien must have left, but I don't know anyone here anymore, and if I had inquired, people would've looked at me with questions I didn't want to answer.

Instead of finding out what I needed to about the Thorne brothers, I ended up back home, sipping on the sparkling champagne that had been delivered when we arrived. My stomach tumbles as I think about the party, but there are still a few hours before we have to leave; that's why I haven't dressed yet.

The moment I put on my costume, there'll be no going back. And I can't think about that right now. I gulp down the last swallow of bubbly before setting the glass on the table, but the moment I rise, I find Paulo at the threshold of my bedroom.

It's my space.

Not his.

Suddenly, my stubbornness takes hold and I want to tell him to leave, but it's no use because this is the man I've agreed to marry. And if I were to do anything to change our arrangement, I would have to give up everything.

Paulo pushes off the door frame before he smirks. "Suppose Mommy Dearest wouldn't know you've been finishing her champagne," he mutters as he enters the room. "Sadly, I might have to inform her of this in case more goes missing." The threat is clear.

"What do you want?" My biting tone doesn't bother him, though. He likes the back and forth, the fight, the tension. He feeds off it and makes it a game.

He settles on my bed, leaning back against the headboard on the same side he slept last night. "I think you need to be nicer to me," he says. "Especially while we're back in the town you lost yourself and where you ended up lying to save yourself."

"What?" My mouth gapes at his accusation, but I can't

allow him to know it's true. I did lie. But Paulo had no idea, I didn't tell him what I did. He must've been doing some digging when he went into town because I never once mentioned Cassian or what happened that night to anyone. And I know Dad wouldn't go back to bad memories, no matter how much he hates the Thornes.

Paulo sighs, but there's a knowing grin on his face. "Sweet little innocent, please don't play me for a fool," he says as he pushes to his feet. "Your little boyfriend is in town, and you didn't think to tell me?"

"What boyfriend? I never once had a boyfriend in school, and when I left here, I walked away from all my friends. Nobody here can tell you about my past." My tone is filled with confidence I don't feel, especially when Paulo arches a brow at me.

He pushes to his feet, his hand reaching out to grip my throat in his large hand. His fingers wrap around my neck, and he tugs me closer, causing me to swallow against the tight hold of his palm.

"Don't fuck with me, druggie whore," he hisses in my face. "Because I will fuck with you, harder, deeper, and much more violent." There's no doubt I would *know* if he were to fuck me, because the man is not only rough, but there's violence in his demeanor that scares me.

When we have been together, that handful of times, he's been calm, but there's always an underlying threat of what could happen if he were to lose control.

"I haven't," I manage to spurt out when he loosens his hold on my neck. The glint in his eye is more than a warning; it's a threat of what's to come if he finds out about Cassian. At least I know Cass won't want me after what I did to him, so there's nothing to worry about.

But even as I think it, I have a feeling this evening is about to explode in a flurry of secrets and truths I'm not prepared for. And some of those will most probably get me killed.

And for a moment, I wonder if it would be so bad.

Not being here.

Paulo leaves me to get ready, and I breathe a sigh of relief.

Time to get into character, and once that's done, it's time to face my past.

The Thorne mansion hasn't changed. Not that I thought it would in the past five years, but seeing it up close, all lit up with decorations, makes it seem almost normal.

We're welcomed as if we were royalty. Champagne is offered, and I quickly take a flute and gulp down a mouthful. The bubbles fizz over my tongue as Paulo presses his fingers against the base of my spine in warning. He watches me all the time. Whenever we're out, the heat of his stare will keep me in line as if I were a puppet on a string, and Paulo grips them oh so tightly.

We move through the crowd, and as I search the sea of people for a familiar face, I realize my heart is thudding against my ribs. He's close; he must be. With every step out into the garden, nervous energy takes hold and doesn't let go. It would've been better if I were here alone, so I could talk to Cassian without Paulo's watchful gaze. But that would never have happened.

"Hello." Mr. Thorne saunters up to us, his hand outstretched to shake Paulo's before he brings mine to his lips. "Welcome to the party. I trust you'll enjoy the evening. We'll have a few games, dancing, and drinks throughout the night."

"Thank you," Paulo responds because I can't find the words. The man who stood in my living room when I was seventeen is before me. Cassian's father. He doesn't recognize me, and if he does, he doesn't say anything.

Once we're alone again, I turn to take in the house from this side of the garden. It's exquisite. Fairy lights trail along the balconies of the bedrooms on the first floor. Lanterns of dancing flames frame the garden, along with a dance floor that has been set up on the grass. But the moment I step on it, I find it's stable enough to feel like an actual concrete floor.

Music blares from the speakers, but my mind is still racing with possibilities. The thought of finally seeing him is at the forefront of my thoughts, and when Paulo leans in, I gasp in surprise.

"I'm going to the restroom," he tells me. "Be a good girl." There's another warning in his tone. Paulo has never trusted me. The past two years have been a struggle. And even though I have no choice but to keep the ring on my finger, deep down, I wish someone would save me from the life I chose.

I set my empty glass down and move through the garden. With every step, I can't help but smile at the decorations. After years of hosting the gala, the Thornes still go out of their way to ensure it's the talk of the town.

A cold shiver trickles down my spine, and when I turn toward the porch which lines the back of the property, my mouth falls open. In the shadows, closest to where the kitchen entrance is, is a form. A man. It's clear that he's staring right at me, his gaze driving a hole through my chest.

The lights are off, which casts him in an eerie glow from the illumination from the party. I'm about to make my way toward him. To demand he talk to me when someone grabs my arm. I turn to find Genevieve, the redhead who I grew up with, smiling at me.

"It's good to see you," she says. "I didn't realize you were back."

"We only arrived yesterday," I inform her. We've never

been friends. She's always wanted a Thorne on her arm, and while her jealousy over my friendship with Cassian was clear, it didn't stop him from choosing to hang out with me rather than her.

"Well, I hope you enjoy the party. Cassian and Finn will most certainly be shocked to see a blast from the past," she remarks before leaving me alone. I want to turn around to see if he's still standing there, but I don't. Instead, I fall into the sea of people and find a few old classmates.

We get into conversation, and for a moment, I relax.

But I know it won't last long.

Because those eyes are still on me.

Cassian

T HE SILVER MOON PEEKS AT ME FROM BETWEEN THE DARK and stormy clouds, reminding me that it's watching. I can't help but smile. The promise of a night of debauchery is what I needed, and now that I'm back in Thorne Haven, I can enjoy the freedom.

The woods beckon with the creak of branches as the howling wind snakes through the trunks. Nature has a mind of her own, and when she's angry, you'd better be careful. Shrugging on my hoodie, I smile, which causes the skeleton mask painted on my face to twist into a grin. There are easily a hundred guests at the party, and the moment I step foot off the porch, onto the soft, lush grass, my gaze zones in on my prey for the night.

The wavy, silky chocolate strands hang to the gentle curve of her bared shoulder blades. She's draped in a long, satin champagne-colored dress that hugs each curve of her frame. Tanned arms are bare, offering me a clear view of the small rose tattoo inked on her shoulder.

The music vibrates through me, the deep bass reminding me of just how fragile we are. If something so small can make the body feel so much, just imagine how an object made of sleek, cool metal can break through the delicate flesh of a human body.

Her laugh echoes across the grass toward me, and I close my eyes, basking in the soft tinkling melody that's made my dick hard each time I've heard it. Following her is something of a hobby, a pastime that's become an addiction.

My father sent me off to London; he ensured I had work to do. Keeping me busy was the plan, but what my family doesn't know about me is that I'm susceptible to human emotions as well. Not the sweet and loving kind, but the dizzying darkness that takes over.

When I was thirteen, I told Dad I was worried. I needed to see a professional. All I got in return were a few sessions and some pills. Talking to a stranger didn't appeal to me after a while, so instead, I enjoyed the calmness and serenity that came with swallowing those little white capsules of calm.

"She's a beaut," my brother Finn says from beside me.

A few years younger than me, and he's most probably had more women than I have. But that doesn't bother me too much. I don't respond to him; instead, I sip the spicy alcohol in my glass. The rum that my father imports is sweet, but there's a hint of spice on the palate, and I have a feeling the woman before me will be just as delicious as my drink.

She moves with her friends as they drift over the lawn to the buffet table. My gaze keeps her in my sights. Her every movement is mine tonight. Only, she doesn't realize it yet.

"You ready for it?" Finn asks.

"Of course," I tell him with a small grin curling my lips. She turns to face the garden, and I get my first look at half of her beautiful face. It's partly hidden by a champagne-colored mask made of lace. The pattern is delicate, like a snowflake, covering her pretty expression. But I don't need to remove it to know what she looks like. "I've been waiting for a long time."

Finn's hand lands on my shoulder in a show of camaraderie. "I know."

When we were growing up, there was a family who lived in town, with a pretty little girl who used to run around in her pink tutu shouting lines from Shakespeare. Her parents were infamous faces, but it was her beauty that brought them a fortune. They plucked the pretty rosebud before she'd bloomed into a beautiful flower and took her to the tainted City of Angels.

"I can't believe what I'm seeing is real," I tell Finn. If Damien were here, he'd be as shocked as I am to learn they'd returned. But I did my research, I investigated the reasons, and now I know why. At first, I wanted her out, but now that I've seen her again, I've changed my mind.

Instead of sending her packing, I'm going to ensure she never leaves Thorne Haven again. She'll be a captive to me, to this town. She walked away before, leaving me with nothing but memories; this time, she'll stay, whether she wants to or not.

Because what she doesn't know is that I will own her.

If she does anything, it will be by my side.

The only problem is, I'm almost certain she hates me as much as I hate her.

It's almost time.

The hands on the clock will hit the eleventh hour, and our game will start. Everyone gathers on the porch and spills out onto the lawn close by. My father takes a cue from his best friend, grinning like a teenager hyped up on something, and speaks into the microphone, informing the crowd that this year, the party will have a special game of hide-and-seek in Thorne Manor.

Usually this is reserved for the Haven party, our neighbors

in town, but when we came to the agreement that the Thornes will host, we went all out.

I glance at Finn, who knows what he must do.

The moment the signal goes, some women race into the house, others into the darkness of the garden to find their hiding places. The adrenaline that's currently racing through my veins has my body alert and my mind at the ready with so many delicious scenarios.

My father glances toward me, already knowing what I plan to do. I'm aching to race inside, to go to her, because I'm certain of where she'll be. Our maids have been positioned in the mansion, keeping an eye on her.

He offers me a nod, and I can't stop my feet from moving into the living room and toward the foyer where I find Joy. She's standing at the foot of the staircase, her smile bright and cheery. She doesn't know what I'm about to do.

"Champagne-colored dress, curly brown hair," I tell her quickly, my voice already turning husky with the thought of finding her on the roof.

"She went up with another girl. They're on the third floor," Joy informs me, and my feet have a mind of their own as I race upstairs, taking them two at a time. "Oh, and Cass," she calls to me from down below, "be careful, would you?"

With a quick nod, I'm moving to the third level of the house, which isn't actually a full floor. It doesn't span the width of the manor. There are only two rooms up here, and with the silence I'm met with, I'm sure it's practically empty.

When I push open the door, it creaks, squeaking along the floorboards of the attic-turned bedroom. It was a space we, as boys, used to bask in because we could be us. No pretenses, no smiles when we didn't want to. It was a safe space.

But tonight, it's nothing of the sort.

"Come out, come out, wherever you are…" I call to the darkness. Even with the sliver of light from the moon, there's not much illumination in the small, cramped space. A shuffle from behind me has me glancing over my shoulder toward the hallway, and I notice a dress that is short, nothing like *hers*, moving toward the steps.

I could catch the girl racing away from me, but my prey is hidden in the depths of this room. A creak from deeper inside causes my head to turn forward, the closet door isn't closed, and I know for a fact it's something we pride ourselves in—tidiness.

"You know," I tell the room, "I used to think that beauty was in the eye of the beholder. I also believed in love and loyalty. And even now, I wonder if that's something you'd stand by." The more I remind myself of what she did, the deeper I walk into the room. Soft breaths filter across the space toward me.

I ponder my move.

This was never my game.

The hide and seek, the hunting, it was more my brothers—Damien and Finn—who reveled in it. I was more of a lurker, a stalker if you want to call me that. I would watch from a distance, allow the prey to come to me. But with her, I want her scared. Desire thrums through my veins. It's as if I can smell the fear which emanates from her like a perfume, filling the confined space.

"Come out, little liar, time to pay your penance," I call in a sing-song tone. A soft gasp sounds when I reach the closet door, and a smile cracks on my face. "In the dark, dark night, the hunter finds his prey," I tell her. "And when he captures her, he'll feast on her fear and devour her flesh."

Shoving the door wide, I listen to how it creaks, and the silky material, the same color as the bubbly that we're serving the guests, comes into view. I reach into the cupboard and fist my hand into the soft strands of brown curls, tugging harshly.

She stumbles from her hiding spot, and those wide chocolate eyes lock on my cold teal ones. Her breath catches when I lean in, inhaling her scent as I grin down at her. I must look like a maniac in my mask. She won't recognize me. It's been years since she even laid eyes on me.

"Are you scared, little liar?" My voice is husky as I question her. I'm only met with a slight nod before I say, "Good. Because you're going to be mine. The next few weeks are going to be your worst nightmare."

"Cassian? Is that you? Why are you doing this?" The fear in her voice drips over me, warming me like molten lava from a raging volcano. Her eyes, widening and her lips, parting as I whisper my mouth over hers. The flavor of the wine she'd been drinking earlier tantalizing me.

"Who else did you think it was, Kalyn?" I question her, with a smirk curling my lips. "Because the moment you stepped foot back in my town, you asked for this. You made yourself a target."

"I-I can't believe you could do this to me," she whimpers, the pure and utter dread in her tone drenches every word. "Why are you doing this when we're—"

"Don't even fucking say we're strangers, or I will show you just how angry I am right now." I release her from my hold, and she stumbles backward. The rules of the game ensure she's mine until our December Winter's Ball. This little game is nothing compared to what she's about to live through.

"Please, just let me explain what happened, why I did what I did. It's better—"

"Get on your fucking knees," I bite out, stepping in her path to the exit. We can hear people on the lower levels, the squeals, and laughs, but they won't come up here because Finn is keeping guard.

For a moment, she hesitates, but the look on my face

must show her I'm not joking around. Slowly, she sinks to the floor, her eyes locked on mine, and I notice the tremble that continually shoots through her.

I smile, and I'm sure it causes the make up on my face to turn sinister. I enjoy the torment I'm causing because when she left, she didn't think twice about what she did to me. And that's okay, I'm over it; the only thing left to do is earn my revenge.

Slowly, torturously, I lift my hand and reach for the gold chain hanging around my neck. I tug at the metal and bring it up over my head until I'm freed from the confines. I flick open the locket and twist it toward her.

Her eyes widen when she sees the two kids standing side by side. And when I glance down at the woman that I'm about to torture for the next six weeks, I offer the dark grin that usually makes others shudder.

Her mouth falls open when she finally looks up, meeting my eyes, and sees *me*. Her expression changes from worry, to excitement, to fear. Just like I knew it would.

"Cassian." My name on her lips is nothing more than fuel to the already raging inferno that's taken hold of me. She did this to me. She made me a monster. And then she says, "I'm sorry."

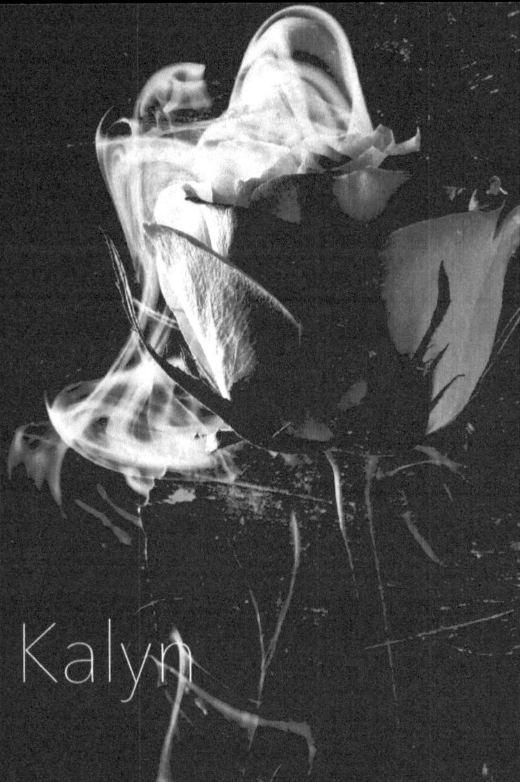

Kalyn

THERE'S NO MORE RUNNING BECAUSE HE IS INCHES from me. The words fall from my lips without me even thinking about them. "I'm sorry." For a long moment, he doesn't respond, and I'm thankful Paulo isn't here right now; he doesn't need to see this. He most definitely doesn't need to know Cassian is here and only a step away, and my heart thuds a nervous rhythm like it usually does around him.

The corner of Cass's mouth tilts, curling into something sinister, especially with the mask on his face. His hand shoots out suddenly, gripping me in much the same way as Paulo did earlier, but this time, this time, I'm burning with both fear and need. "Sorry?" The sneer that graces his handsome face twists my gut into a knot that makes it difficult to breathe. "Do you think that will fix what you said about me?"

My mouth opens, then closes because, to be honest, *no*, I don't think it will fix anything between us. But even as his fingers dip against my skin, I know there's no other man who can make me feel like he does.

"There is nothing you can say or do that will fix what you told your parents I did, especially in your father's eyes." His words slam right into my chest, and it makes it hard to breathe.

"I-I didn't..." Words fail me because there is nothing I can tell him that could fix us. Fix what I did.

"You didn't mean to fuck my life into the ground with your lie? My father had me in therapy after you left. I spent months trying to convince him that I wasn't some junkie addict," Cassian spits angrily, leaning into me, his body so close, I can feel him vibrate with rage. His fingers dig into my throat, and I'm so thankful we're alone, hidden from the crowd. "Is that why you're back now, with that fancy man on your arm to show me just how well you're doing without me?"

My mouth once again falls open, but no words come out. *How can I tell him how much I cared when I nearly shattered his life to pieces?* Thankfully his father has sway in this town and was able to squash the claims I made.

"Paulo has nothing to do with this, with us," I bite out. I don't know why I'm defending a man who's holding me hostage, but I want to show Cassian I'm stronger than he thinks. Even though the truth is so far from what he can see. "I came home because I needed to do what my father had asked of me."

"Oh? I'm sure that's all that's brought you back here. Or was it because you wanted to see if I'd finally fuck you?" The evil glint in his eyes is nothing like the Cassian I had come to know, come to love. This man before me is different. When he was younger, there was always happiness in his gaze; now, there's merely a ghost of the boy I remember.

"Fuck you, Cassian," I bite out through clenched teeth, but he only chuckles because I'm sure he can see just how much I do want him—to touch me, to kiss me, and yes, to fuck me. Shaking my head, I glance out the window and focus on the garden behind him before I sigh. "There is so much more to what happened that night," I tell him, hoping he'll allow me to explain.

"Were you that obsessed with me you lied and told them I wanted you too? That I would give you something to keep you high so I could get in a quick fuck?" He throws the words at me, slicing a gaping hole in my chest. I can't be angry, though. I was the young girl following him around like a lost puppy. But then again, he was always there for me to run to.

Cassian pushes me away, releasing my neck from his grip. He spins on his heel and glares at me from over his shoulder. I know I deserve this because I started it. I agreed when my father accused him of something heinous. I should've stopped it. I could have, but I didn't.

I was guilty.

I was embarrassed.

And I fucked up.

"I didn't mean to," I finally whisper, but Cassian only shakes his head at my admission. "I really didn't." This time, I'm up on my feet, finding courage I didn't think I had. When I reach for Cassian, he shies away from me, but the moment my fingertips land on his arm, the electric current between us is nothing short of cataclysmic.

He doesn't realize that I didn't actually *say* anything that night. He was always there for me, and I was nothing more than a child with issues.

My parents couldn't deal with it. That night they asked, they forced me to say something, to give them a truth I didn't want to. In my stupidity, in my swirling mind, I admitted to a lie—I screamed my agreement at Dad before I realized what I had said, and now I must live with the consequences. I look at Cassian then and finally voice the truth, "I didn't mean to say—"

Cassian spins on his heel, his eyes latching onto mine,

holding me hostage as he glares at me. "I don't want to hear your excuses, Kalyn." His jaw clenches, rage simmering just below the surface of those ocean eyes. "After everything we've been through, I've always been a gentleman to you, and yet, you throw me under the bus because your fucking high was far too fucking sweet to come down from."

The hate he's spewing has been rightly earned. I can't apologize because what I did was more than wrong; it was unacceptable. I allowed the lie about him to flourish without stopping it. I knew if I had told my father that I willingly went out to lose myself, he wouldn't believe me. They always saw me as the *good girl*. So, I lied, only to wake up to a nightmare.

"I cared about you so much." My voice is merely a whisper, and I wonder how he can hear me, but Cassian has always heard me. Even in the deepest, darkest of nights, he would listen to me.

It was as if we were in tune with each other. He moved, I moved. He spoke, I finished his sentence. But the link was broken, and it was because of me.

"Caring for someone means you stand by them like I did with you all those years. You don't lie about their intentions." His voice is husky with emotion, and all I want to do is pull him into my arms and cry.

But I don't, instead, I look at him and say, "I didn't mean to."

"But you still did it, and that's never going to change," he throws back in response. "You're a liar, little Kaly, a little liar."

"I-I... I'm truly sorry, Cassian. I didn't mean to hurt you." And even now, after all these years, my heart cracks. I blink, and the tears trickle from my lashes, creating a long, burning trail down my cheeks. When I open my eyes once more, I meet those teal orbs that always offered me solace. Now all they gift me is chaos.

Cass takes a step closer to me until he's in my personal space. His body looms over mine, the heat of him scorching me, and I welcome the flames. He leans in, his mouth closing the distance between us, and for a moment, I think he's going to kiss me. And shockingly, *or not*, I want him to.

But he doesn't press his lips to mine; instead, he stops at my ear. "If you think this is over," he threatens, "you're sorely mistaken, little liar." A shudder wracks my frame, his hot breath leaving goosebumps in its wake when he pushes away from me. "That piece of shit you're engaged to," Cassian says, the contempt in his tone is clear, "he has nothing on me. Because I have my own brand of punishment, and when I get you alone and trust me, I will, I'll make sure you beg and plead."

He lifts his hand, cupping my face tightly, then trails his touch down to my neck before he grips it harshly. His fingers dig into the skin, and I wonder if he'll mark me. If when I wake up tomorrow morning, I'll be bruised by his touch.

"I will make you want nothing more than my cock in that little cunt," Cassian vows. "I'll finally give you what you need, and I don't give a shit if you're married or not. Because when I take you, I'm going to make you feel me, and only me. And when I walk away, you'll always feel the emptiness of me."

He turns to leave, and for a second, I want to call out to him to tell him to stay. I want to explain, to try and fix things, but I know it's no use because he's convinced himself that making me hurt will make this right.

Only, he doesn't know just how much I'm already suffering.

Kalyn

WHEN I REJOIN THE PARTY, I FIND PAULO STANDING with a few people I haven't met before. The infamous gala has always brought strangers to town who want to experience the parties of Thorne Haven.

I step up beside him, still shaking from the encounter with Cassian. My feelings for him haven't changed. There is no doubt I still love him. As I always have.

His hand lands on my lower back, a warning in his firm touch, even though there's a smile on his face. It's a look he's perfected in front of strangers. He likes to ensure the façade is visible to those who might see the truth. "I couldn't find you," he whispers, keeping his voice low so I'm the only one who can hear him.

"I'm sorry." There's no way I can tell him where I was. My mind is still a mess; my heart, on the other hand, knows what it wants, what it's always wanted.

Cassian isn't an old teenage crush. He's the man I love, and I know I'll never stop loving him. I glance around only to find Finn watching us from a distance. His dark gaze pierces me when I lock my stare on his.

The corner of his mouth quirks, and he tips his head to the side as he regards me. Moments later, Cassian saunters up beside his brother. In his hand, he's carrying a bottle of what I can only guess is vodka—his drink of choice. He watches me for a long while.

Paulo drags me through the crowd, his anger radiating off him in waves. We get to the bar where he orders a white wine for me and a double shot of bourbon for himself.

"If you try to act the innocent little whore here," he threatens in a low hiss once everyone around us is out of earshot, "I'll make sure you never forget acting like one."

I glance up into black eyes that hold contempt at my response to him earlier.

"Everyone enjoying the party?" Finn's voice comes from behind us, breaking the glare Paulo's pinned me with as he turns to the man interrupting his rage.

He turns to face Finn, a smile gracing his perfectly carved face. "It's a beautiful home you have," he tells Finn. "I was just telling my fiancée it would be great to have something similar once we've decided where to settle down after the wedding."

Finn throws his glance my way, his dark brow infinitesimally arching, but I don't respond. "Well, Thorne Haven is a town that will most certainly burrow itself under your skin," he tells Paulo. "It will feel like home after a few days."

"Perhaps," Paulo responds, picking up his drink and taking a sip, his gaze sizing up the man before him. "And you are?"

"Oh, I'm a Thorne," Finn says but doesn't offer his name. "This is one of the annual parties my family throws. I trust you'll enjoy the rest of your evening." Without waiting for a response from Paulo, Finn offers a nod and leaves us.

"Is that the bastard you were fucking when you were a kid?" Paulo grits as he grabs my arm and hauls me through the crowd once more.

"I wasn't fucking anyone." My response is a gasp when my back hits the wall. With everyone dancing and enjoying themselves, they don't take note of what's happening.

Paulo leans in, his lips at my ear, and that's when I feel heat burning through me. Teal eyes are locked on us from the second-floor bedroom balcony, where Cassian is standing; he's watching every fucking move we make.

He lifts the bottle he's holding to his lips and takes a long swig before he lowers it and pins me with a stare so fierce, so filled with anger and desire, I don't hear what Paulo says.

When a hand grips my hair, tugging until tears sting my eyes, I'm quickly brought back to my situation.

"Are you listening to me?"

"Sorry, I—"

"We're leaving," he announces. "I'm done with you acting like a slut around men. Tonight, you'll take a double dose." The promise is clear, and as we move to the door, my stomach sinks to my feet, and my heart splinters.

If only I'd never left Thorne Haven. If only I hadn't lied about Cassian. If only I could make him see just how much I love him.

But none of that is possible.

I can never have the man I love.

And I can never find solace in this town.

Cassian

My head throbs as I lean my elbows on the kitchen table. Perhaps my idea of drowning my sorrows last night wasn't one of my better ideas. The coffee that's steaming from my mug doesn't offer solace; instead, it has me wanting to puke my guts up. Last night after I left Kalyn, I thought I'd find a pretty girl to use as I wish, but instead, I abused a bottle of vodka up on the roof while watching the party below.

I watched Kalyn and her fiancé as they moved through the crowd. And with every touch of his hand on her body, I swallowed back the clear alcohol and allowed my jealousy to rage and my anger to burn. My temper had taken hold of me last night when I finally had her all to myself. But even in that cloud of red, her scent was so familiar, I wanted to drown in it.

She's been a drug to me since she was fifteen, when her family moved here. She was too young for me then, even though we're three years apart. But then I realized she had more demons that I couldn't eradicate.

I didn't want her to have to deal with her pain as well as mine. So instead of telling her about what I'd been going through, I allowed her to distract me from my thoughts. And she did. Everything about her had pulled me in; I was a guy lost to a girl who was his savior. Only, she didn't know it.

Her sheltered upbringing was refreshing, and when I first spoke to her, I realized she wasn't like the girls from Thorne Haven; she was different. I was enthralled by her sass and wit.

I wanted nothing more than to lock her in a glass case to keep her safe. I didn't want this world to change her, to make her hard and cold. But it did so anyway. When her grandmother died, she dove headfirst into the world of Thorne Haven, being corrupted by the partying and drugs.

Even though I tried to help, tried to steer her clear of the bullshit I was so accustomed to, the lure of forgetting, of ignoring the pain with the sweet high was too much, so instead of being the boyfriend she could've had, I was the savior she didn't want.

"You look like shit." Finn's amused tone comes from the doorway, and I look up to find my brother leaning against the door frame, arms folded.

"Thanks," I throw back before swallowing the coffee I'd been pondering over. "Good party last night." My voice is croaky as I speak.

"It was," Finn agrees as he enters the room, heading straight for the coffee machine. Once he has his mug, he joins me at the table. "You get to talk to her last night?" he asks the question I've been waiting for.

Nodding, I answer, "I did. She had the audacity to apologize to me. As if saying *sorry* is going to make it better." I lift my gaze when he doesn't respond, and I find my brother's wary stare on mine. "What?"

"I don't know, I just..." Finn shakes his head, running his fingers through his hair, before he continues, "I think there's more to why she's back than meets the eye."

"Like what?" I challenge, leaning back against the chair. I narrow my gaze, focusing on him as I wait for him to explain. I'm not sure what Kalyn could be hiding. She seems happy enough with her new man, and I'm still here, left in the background with her fake apologies and fake smiles.

"I don't know what, not yet. But I intend to find out." Finn drinks his coffee before he speaks once more, "I noticed something strange last night with that man on her arm."

"Strange?" This piques my interest. All I remember from last night was drowning my anger in vodka. Yes, I did watch her for a long time as the night wore on, but when Paulo pulled her in to plant a long kiss on her lips, I walked away, just like she did that last time I saw her all those years ago.

"Don't worry about it," Finn says as he pushes to his feet. "Once I've figured it out, I'll—"

"Tell me, Finn," I urge, needing to know what my brother is talking about. There are so many secrets that already fill the walls of our town, but right now, I'm done with games. I need the truth.

"The fiancé," Finn starts, "I don't like the look of him, of them together. There's something not right about him." There's a cautious tone to his voice, one that's not always present in my youngest brother, and that's why I take note.

"Like what, though?" This has me leaning forward, my elbows on the table because he has me intrigued. If there is something off about Mr. Fiancé, then I want all the details.

"I don't know." Finn pulls out his cell phone, unlocks it, and hands me the device. There, on the screen, is a photo of Kalyn and Paulo, which I now know is her *fiancé's* name. They're at a party in the Hollywood Hills. But it's not the bright lights and champagne that catch my attention; it's his hold on her arm. The way his fingers dig into her flesh, the way she smiles isn't genuine; it's... pained.

My gaze snaps to Finn's. "Let's get this fucker," I murmur,

anger taking hold, the need to hurt him burning through my veins. Yes, I do want Kalyn to pay for what she did, but if anyone is going to hurt her, it will be me. Not some piece of shit who thinks he can rule her life. "He must have something on her. There has to be a reason she hasn't walked away because if there's one thing I know about Kaly, she wouldn't sit around with a bastard ruling her life."

"She has too much fire," Finn agrees, knowing the girl I've been obsessed with all my life. And he knows I'm right. "I think it's time we call Harris," he tells me, but I'm already pressing the call button on my phone and holding the device to my ear.

"Harris, I need your help." It's time to figure out why my girl is back, what's brought her here, and who the bastard is that she's agreed to marry. "I need everything on Kalyn Narro since she left Thorne Haven. Also, there's a fiancé in the picture, and I don't like the look of him."

"I'm on it. Do you have a name for him?"

"Paulo?" I offer easily. Even saying his name leaves a bitter taste in my mouth. Finn's right. I didn't notice it at the party because I was too focused on Kalyn. If I had stopped losing myself in the bottle of vodka, I would've realized there was something off about him.

"I'll have something for you in about an hour." Harris is good, he's been with us for years, mostly doing work for Dad, but now that we're working at Thorne Industries, he's done a lot of deep diving research for us.

I hang up and glance at Finn. "He said an hour," I tell him. "I'm going to see her." I'm already grabbing my keys from the holder when I feel Finn's glare burning a hole through me. I look at him. "What?"

"You're going to go there, where the asshole is playing house?"

The thought of Kalyn stuck in there with him doesn't sit well with me. Perhaps I should let this go for a while, but I can't. Not after I've seen the evidence.

"If I go there as an old friend, he won't know shit," I tell Finn. "Also, he was in our house; I can play the welcome to Thorne Haven card." He looks dubious when I say this, but I'm not giving up on my idea.

"You just want to see her." Finn grins. "You're so easy to read," he informs me with a chuckle while he shakes his head.

"I need to make sure she's okay. If he was angry about me stealing her time at the party, he could've done something to her."

For a long while, Finn stares at me, but after a few moments, he nods, knowing I'm right. I don't trust a man who'll hit a woman. I may want her to pay for her little lies, but deep down, my feelings for her are still soul-stealing. She's always been a force in my life, in my mind, and at times I certainly act like an obsessive stalker when it comes to Kalyn.

She's always brought out my possessive nature. Especially when we were in school. But this time, it's different. I'm doing it for her safety. The memory of her in her school uniform has me remembering all the bastards I had to warn off her. She didn't realize just how popular she was with the guys. But it was me who ensured they steered clear of her. Even though I didn't publicly claim her as mine, they knew not to touch her.

"Be careful," Finn warns, drawing my attention back to him and away from the past. I make my way out to my silver Audi R8 with my brother's warning ringing in my ears. By the time I'm out on the road, my nervous energy has turned to the need for vengeance, this time not aimed at Kalyn. This time, I want that bastard to fucking pay for hurting her.

It doesn't take long for me to reach the Narro house and press the buzzer outside the enormous black metal gates.

"Hello?" Kalyn's voice comes through the speaker, and my chest tightens with the need to be near her. As angry as I am at her, she still holds my heart, only, she doesn't know it.

"It's me," I say, and I don't miss the soft gasp that filters through to me. "Open the gate, Kaly." I don't have to command her to do anything because I know if I sat here long enough, she'd let me in.

Once the heavy gates swing open, I pull up the drive and

stop right outside the door. Exiting the car, I make my way around and up the steps that lead to the door. By the time I reach it, it swings open, and I'm met with those cocoa eyes.

"What are you doing here?" she asks before I can get a word out. "You shouldn't have come here." The fear in her voice only sets me on edge because if she's scared of him, what Finn and I thought about him is correct.

"Let me in, or I'll cause a scene," I tell her. For a long moment, she stares at me before she steps aside.

"Fine. But you can't stay long; he's in the shower." Her hiss is tense, her gaze darting to the staircase before swinging back to me. "What do you want, Cassian?"

"Tell me something, little liar," I start, taking a step toward her, expecting her to move back, but she doesn't. With me, she stands her ground, and it only makes my cock hard. "Is he doing something to you? Is he hurting you?" I keep my voice low, so if the asshole decides to walk out from wherever he's hiding, he won't hear me.

Those pretty eyes widen in shock at my question; her mouth pops open into an O that makes my blood heat with desire. "You should leave."

"I asked you a fucking question. If you don't answer me, I'll go up there and ask him." The threat is purely that, to scare her into telling me. I wouldn't put her in danger, but I need her to be honest with me.

"He's... controlling. He makes sure I stay healthy." Her lie is clear. I could always tell when Kalyn was lying to me, and right now, it's so fucking obvious, bells are going off in my head. "Please leave!"

Kalyn

HE LOOKS AT ME FOR A LONG TIME BEFORE HE IMPLORES, "Meet me this afternoon, tell him you're going to see Gen or someone else from school." My stomach tumbles, and my stomach flutters with hummingbird wings. It's been far too long since I've felt these emotions. Need. Want. Desire. And love.

"Cass—"

"Do it," he orders before he spins on his heel and steps over the threshold. A quick glance over his shoulder and those teal eyes penetrate my armor, sending me spiraling when he says, "I need to see you. Give me an hour. Tonight, at the cemetery." And then he's gone, and I'm left alone a wildly thudding heart. Leaning on the door frame, I watch his car snake down the drive and disappear through the ornate gates that my father had custom-made—when we still had money.

I don't know how I'll get away from Paulo's watchful gaze, but as Cassian said, I could just tell him I'm going to see Gen. She may not be my best friend, but maybe I could use her name for now, and apologize later. Hell knows we're all not perfect, especially in this pristine little town. There is a darkness that seems to hover over it.

"Kalyn?" Paulo's tone startles me, causing me to spin around and find him at the top of the steps. "What are you doing?"

"Just enjoying the fresh air and the view." Even though it's a lie, he can't dispute it because the view of the town from our front door is spectacular.

"Come inside," Paulo orders, his voice terse with annoyance, and I close the door before a fight breaks out. I never realized until now how little things are eating away at me. Small things he does make me anxious.

"I'd like to go out this evening to see an old friend," I tell him as I make my way up the steps. "She's the only girl I really know from school." I tack on, making sure I mention that the friend in question is *female.*

"You have an hour," he tells me easily, and my anxiety untwists itself as I breathe deeply. He doesn't take too much notice of me as he turns away after throwing out the order, so I allow myself to smile.

I nod mostly to myself, and I say, "Sure."

The moment to face Cassian again has come. Paulo allowed me to leave the house, which was surprising even after he said it was okay. Most times, he'll change his mind on a whim, and that normally leaves me with nothing to do or requires me to fulfill his needs.

I'm standing at the entrance of the cemetery, trying to build up the courage to walk inside. I saw Cassian's car, so I know he's here, but still, my nerves have taken hold.

Taking a few steps through the gate that hangs open from being broken, I enter the cemetery. My feet move of their own accord because my stomach is twisting in knots as I move closer to the center, where I know a mausoleum sits in the middle of the graves like a king overlooking his countrymen.

"I didn't think you'd make it." Cassian's voice comes out of the darkness, startling me. I spin around to find him sitting on a gravestone, his arms folded across his chest as if he's comfortable in a place like this.

Thorne Haven holds many secrets. The town itself has seen some intriguing events, but nothing I know too much about. However, I know Cassian's family has been here since the beginning. They founded this town with the Havens, and if I were to guess, there are still many hidden truths that lie buried with those who passed away long ago.

Granted, this was the place we would spend most of our time in. I found it calming, and I would find peace amongst death. I remember asking him about Thorne Haven many times in the years of our friendship, and he would always brush it off. I don't know the entire history, but I have a feeling Cassian's family has hidden secrets he doesn't want to come out.

"I almost didn't," I tell him honestly. I don't move closer to where he is, I stick to the path, so if I needed to run for whatever reason, I could find my way out.

Even though the moon shines down on us, there's not much visibility where we are. Cassian's dressed in black, with a white tank top from what I can tell as his hoodie hangs off his left shoulder.

"What did you want?" I ask, wanting to get this over with, but in the same breath, wanting him to keep me here. If he were to kidnap me, perhaps I would be free of the man who's truly holding me hostage.

"Tell me what he is doing to you, Kaly?" Cassian asks, his voice cold, like ice trickling down my spine, and I can't stop the shiver that trails from the top of my head to the tips of my toes.

I want to lie. It's my first instinct because I know Cass, and if I were to tell him about my life, something bad would happen. Not to Paulo, but to me and Cassian. Deep down, all I want is for the boy who once held my heart to take it once more and keep it safe.

"Nothing," I finally lie to Cassian, and my heart cracks.

His anger is palpable; it's a force to be reckoned with because the moment he moves, I'm nothing but prey in his eyes. His grip on my chin is unyielding as he tugs me to look at him. There's no escaping the teal glare that's holding me hostage.

"Don't you dare fucking lie to me," Cassian grits angrily, his teeth clenching in frustration as he regards me. The blaze in his eyes sends heat coursing through my veins, and my thighs squeeze together.

"I can't talk about it with you," I finally respond after a long silence. He doesn't say anything; he doesn't move, still holding onto my chin as if it were a lifeline.

"I want you away from him," Cassian declares as if it's the easiest thing in the world to do. I can't just walk away from Paulo, not when he's paying for my father's treatments.

I shake my head slowly. He doesn't understand. "Cassian—"

"Don't fucking give me that. I don't give a shit anymore." Anger emanates off him as he releases me and turns his back on me. I watch him as turmoil so clearly twists inside him. I've never seen him like this, and I want to go to him, to wrap my arms around his waist and press my body against his. For so long, I've wanted to be his, to have him be mine, but it's too late.

I shake my head and force myself to make my way to him. His heat sizzles through me as I near him. Reaching for him, I press my palm against his back. "There's no way I can leave without him losing his mind. There are too many variables that hang in the balance if I were to decide to do it."

"Then I'll make you," he threatens, his head turning, his gaze burning into me as he watches me. "I'll find a way." My chest tightens, and my heart thuds against my ribs. He's always had it. Cassian has had my heart since I first laid eyes on him.

"There's no way, Cassian. I cannot just walk away from promises I've made." My plea falls on deaf ears when he chuckles. He's beyond rational thought at this point, and I realize I should've stayed home. Cassian Thorne isn't used to being told no, but right now, I'm defying him more than I ever have. "My life is difficult, complicated. And no amount of money is going to change that," I add on, because I know he will throw out a comment about paying for something to be done.

"Oh, my little liar," he whispers as he turns to fully face me. "When I want something, I always make it happen."

And there it is, Cassian's overconfidence.

A small smile graces my lips. It's true, and I know it. He's always been someone who's gotten what he wants. Most times, things are easy to capture, but this time, it's different. I meet his gaze and say, "But this time, you're too late."

"Fuck being late, Kaly," he murmurs, stalking toward me so quickly, I step back and slam into the wall of the mausoleum. The cold concrete ensures I can't run away; I'm nothing more than a hostage to Cassian right now.

He stops when he's inches from me, his large, looming frame caging me in, and an icy shiver of awareness trickles down my spine. Cassian would never hurt me, that much I know, but the way he's looking at me right now makes everything I know about him fall into question.

My body heats at his nearness as it usually does, and the air sparks with electric desire. His eyes dance with need as he regards me, a smile slowly tilting the corners of his mouth.

"If you think for one second you can walk back into my town and tell me you're not mine, then you have another thing coming, little liar," he informs me confidently. "I'm going to ensure you're in my possession soon, and when you are, you're not returning to that piece of shit you call a fiancé."

I want to scream at him.

I want to tell him to leave me alone.

But it would be a lie.

I've always wanted to belong to Cassian Thorne. For years, I prayed he'd wake up and finally lay claim to me. And now that I have a heavy diamond ring on my finger, he's chosen this moment to finally declare I'm his.

"You need to walk away from this, Cass. Please, I don't want you getting hurt," I plead, stepping toward him, which only seems to make the fire burn brighter in his eyes.

He leans in, his face now a hairsbreadth away from mine. "I'll never give up on you, Kalyn. You may have made sure I want you to pay for what you did, but I'll never allow a woman in my life to hurt because of a man."

There's no lie in his words.

Cassian is a good guy. So are his brothers. But Cass was always the one who stole my attention. In a room full of people, it was always him. And now that I'm all grown up, it's still him.

The thought brings a lump to my throat, and tears burn my eyes as I consider walking away from this man for good. If I were to tell him right now to give it up, to finally say goodbye to me, I know he'd respect my choice.

But when I open my mouth, I can't find the words to tell him so. He watches me for a long while before he drops his head, and his lips feather along mine. It's not a real kiss, but the contact is there.

His warm breath fans over my face as he speaks, "You may think you escaped the first time you walked out of Thorne Haven, but you can't tell me you spent the last five years not thinking of me."

"I—I can't admit to anything because you know it will be a lie," I throw back easily. While I was gone, he was the only person who invaded my mind every single day, it's embarrassing, but also, it reminds me just how much I love him.

"Then you will have no qualms when I make my move." The underlying promise is there. He's going to do something stupid, and I'm most certainly not going to fight him.

I know I won't.

He knows I won't.

But I wonder just what will happen when Paulo finds out the truth.

"Soon, little liar," Cassian promises before he saunters from the graveyard, leaving me in the dark to ponder what's about to happen. My life is once again about to blow up, and I have no control over it.

Kalyn

ROLLING OVER IN BED, I CURL INTO THE SHEETS AND keep my eyes closed. The dream that woke me lingers, and I think back on it, remembering one of the worst but also most beautiful moments of my life.

I've been crying for hours. The drive back from my grandmother's house is long, silent, and filled with my pain which feels as if the world is crashing down on me. The grief is debilitating. My lungs struggle to do their job while my chest tightens every time I try to pull in air.

When I close my eyes, I see her, and when I open them, all I see before me is a dark cloud that hangs heavily over me. As if my life is under a constant state of rain. My heart is broken, and I don't know how I'm going to get through this without the high which always calms me.

As we pull into the drive, I notice Cassian's car parked in the street, but I don't say anything to my parents. They wanted me to stay in tonight, but all I can think about is getting out of my head, out of remembering what happened, getting drunk, or something far stronger than Cassian will like.

The kids at school all do drugs, well, most of them, but I've only ever dabbled with a joint or two. But right now, all I want is to forget. To stop thinking and replaying the past few days. She didn't even know me before she took her final breath, and that's what's cracking through my chest, a tight fist wrapping around my heart and squeezing.

I want to forget.

I want to get lost in a high that will clear my mind of the memories and images that have shattered my heart into a million pieces.

The slam of a door snaps me from the thoughts, and I look up to find my parents waiting on me. We make our way into the house, and I head straight for my bedroom, where I wait until I hear my parents going to bed.

Climbing out of my window has become second nature, and it doesn't take me long to find Cass still parked in the same spot. I slip into the passenger seat of his car, and before he can say anything, I break down.

Cassian doesn't think twice, he pulls me into his lap, and soon,

I'm straddling him. His arms wrap around me, and he warms me with his calm affection. He doesn't ask questions, he doesn't say anything, he allows me to cry, to expel my pain through my tears.

I don't know how long we sit there, but when I finally look up into his affectionate gaze, my heart stutters. He doesn't move, he doesn't even breathe, and that's when I realize how close we really are.

"I-I'm sorry." My voice is croaky when I speak, but he doesn't laugh. He merely lifts his hands, cups my cheeks, and swipes the tears from my face.

"There isn't any reason to apologize," Cassian tells me, his voice even, calm. My solace. "What happened?"

I open my mouth to speak, but the moment I want to say something, my throat closes, and I choke up once more.

"You don't have to tell me," he says softly, placing a kiss on my forehead before he looks me in the eye. "When you're ready, I'll be here. I'll always be here. I'll always come for you."

"M-my grandmother," I mumble the words, but I don't need to finish my sentence. He knows me. He finishes my sentences most times, and this is one of those moments I'm thankful for our connection.

"I'm so sorry, my little star," he coos, and I watch as his long, dark lashes flutter against his cheeks. Cassian kisses my cheek before he pulls me closer. He hugs me to him. He holds me through another bout of my sobs, and even though I'm wracked with heartache, it's Cassian who keeps me afloat.

It's in this moment, right here, in the dark, that I realize I'm *in love with my best friend. A boy who's three years my senior. A boy who makes my heart tumble wildly. And a boy I know I'll love forever.*

It's been a few days since the secret meeting with Cassian in the cemetery, and I've been avoiding going anywhere near Thorne Manor, or town. I'm still anxious about being back in this beautifully gothic town that gave me a second chance when I needed it most. Even though I should be less stressed since Cassian and I have had it out, mostly, I feel ill at ease.

The familiar thump in my brain confirms last night was either a late one or one of the evenings that Paulo felt I needed something more to get me to bed. It happens more often now than it did when we met.

Even though he's put on a smile, offered his help, there's something deeply evil about the man who sleeps beside me. And even though I have no way of getting out now, I know I'm in danger.

My family comes first. Dad's health is my main priority, so if Paulo says he'll happily help us, I believe him. I trust he'll ensure my father's medical trials go as planned. Even though I haven't ever asked where the money comes from, I gratefully accept it because I know Dad needs it.

Pushing from the bed, I stand on shaky legs, and my head spins for a moment before I focus on the sun streaming through the window. I lift my hands and find them trembling, as usual, before I've had my coffee.

At times it feels like I need a high to get through the day. It's my own fault. This is what I've done to myself since I fell down the rabbit hole when I was sixteen, and I've never escaped. The feeling of flying, of freedom, of not feeling the pain has always been far too alluring.

So, I did it.

I allowed myself to jump headfirst into the abyss, and I haven't pulled myself out of it. Cassian tried, so many times, but I didn't allow him to fully save me. Instead, I gave him a false sense of security. I made him feel like a hero when he was nothing more than a life raft. As soon as I let go of him, I fell under again.

Taking in the brightness of the room, I can't help but groan. I'm almost certain I closed the curtains last night, but perhaps I didn't. Spending all my time in the house probably isn't the best thing to do, but I know if I were to head into town, I'd probably run into a Thorne or one of the Haven brothers. Even though I love Thorne Haven, I've always felt as if I'm an outsider. The only person who welcomed me was *him*.

I make my way to the bathroom and freshen up before I pad barefoot down to the kitchen. I find Paulo at his laptop when I step through the door.

"I figured you'd sleep all day," he remarks when I head

to the coffee machine and flick it on as I settle a mug underneath. Instead of answering, I focus on getting my caffeine.

Last night was one of *those* nights, where he was angry because he's stuck here, when he wants to be in LA. Even though I didn't need him here, he insisted on coming, but in the end, it's my fault. Like everything else is.

"I'm going to head into town today," I say, but I don't look at him. My body isn't strong anymore. I don't have the fight in me that I used to have. So, I focus on my mug that's now filled with dark liquid.

"And where are you intending on spending the day?" Paulo questions, his voice lilting with dark intent. If I were to tell him I'm hoping to see Cassian, I'll be bound to the bed upstairs and high on whatever he decides to inject into my veins.

"My friend, Genevieve," I lie. She's not a friend, merely an acquaintance I grew up hating. Not because she did anything to me, but because she was best friends with the Thornes. Her connection to them turned into something more when she and the eldest brother, Damien, started hooking up. And then, they were all in her sights.

But, as much as I can't stand her, she's a lesser evil than Paulo. So I close my eyes and pray he doesn't delve deeper into my reasoning.

"I don't want you out late," he says, but the clicking of

the keys on his laptop is evidence that he's not bothered because I mentioned the name of a woman. "Perhaps bring her here," he suggests, his voice turning gentle, and I know why he's saying that.

There's no hiding that the man I agreed to marry cheats. I've seen him with other women. Granted, it was when we were in LA, and at those parties, he'd always ensured I wasn't focused on what he was doing. He knew when to give me something to keep me compliant. Whether it was in my drink or a pill, Paulo was well versed in keeping women at his beck and call.

Most times, I thought I was imagining things. At least, that's what he used to tell me I was doing.

"I'll see if she'd like to have dinner with us," I offer before sipping my drink. My gaze lingers on the garden behind the house because I can't look at my soon-to-be husband. If I do, I'll break down and cry.

Cassian saw us together at the party, and deep down, I wonder if he was jealous. Most people assume we're happily engaged, but they don't truly know me. Cassian does, and he surely knows the truth. And that is, I'm a prisoner in my own home. The pain I've endured, the drugs that have been forced upon me, are not of my choosing, not anymore.

When I wanted to go to rehab, I begged my parents. They agreed; only when Paulo walked in and promised them the world, pledged to pay for my dad's treatments, did I realize my life would never be the same.

And even then, I didn't fight it.

I played the dutiful fiancée, which brings me here, to Thorne Haven, to a place I never thought I'd see again. And it brings me back to why my heart is broken.

"Don't be out late," Paulo says again, but he's still working, so all I do is offer a nod and hastily make my way to the bedroom to change. I pull on a pair of jeans and a long, flowing tee, which covers my slight curves.

I'm no longer the vivacious girl Cassian will remember. Now, I'm nothing more than a waif that has a bad past. In the car, I pull away from the house with my breath still filling my lungs, trying to ignore the fact that I'm sure Paulo is watching from one of the windows.

I don't race, though. Instead, I take a slow drive down the cobblestone driveway until I reach the gate, which slides open. Once I'm on the road, I put my foot on the gas and head away from town.

It's time I came face-to-face with Cassian again, but this time, I'm going to be the one calling the shots. Before I head home later, I'll go see Gen, talk to her, and pray she doesn't tell me to go to hell.

I don't have friends in this town.

There isn't anyone I can run to when I need something. It used to only be Cass, and when he was busy, I would face whatever it was alone. High. But alone.

By the time I pull up to Thorne Manor, I'm shaking like a leaf. Perhaps I should've eaten something before coming here, but spending one more moment with Paulo would've sent me over the edge. And that would've only led to more drugs, which I don't need right now.

What I do need is the brutal truth.

Exiting the car, I find Finn sauntering out of the house with keys swinging on his index finger. "Oh," he says, a smile playing on his lips, "now this is a sight I didn't expect so early in the morning."

"I need to see Cass." My voice breaks, the croakiness causing the words to sound more pained than confident, and I clear my throat in the hopes he didn't notice.

"He's inside. Kitchen," Finn says before saluting me. "Good luck." By the time he disappears, I'm nervous once more, but I force myself to head into the house that's brought me so much happiness but also so many tears.

Time to face my past.

Cassian

WHEN FOOTSTEPS SOUND BEHIND ME, I TURN around, and I'm struck speechless. Standing on the threshold of my kitchen is a girl, no, a woman, I didn't expect to see.

"What are you doing here?"

She winces at my question, and I realize it sounded as if I were accusing her. Perhaps I am. Maybe I want her to feel pain just because I was hurt at what she said about me.

It's petty.

I know it is, but I can't stop myself from feeling like that, as if she needs to pay. But then when I look at her, when I remember what happened the night of the party, I realize she's already paying.

"I needed to see you," she finally answers, her voice taut, her hands tangling as she regards me from under her long dark lashes. She's so beautiful, it hurts to look at her; it's as if looking directly at the sun. The brightness is just too much for the naked eye.

"Why? Isn't your fiancé going to get angry and jealous you're here, still wanting me while you're wearing his ring?" My words hurt her, it's clear on her pretty face, but I don't take it back.

Maybe I'm the jealous one.

It's me who needs to rein it in.

"Cassian, I'm not with him for love," she admits, stepping closer to where I'm leaning against the countertop. She stops near me, close enough for me to inhale her sweet scent—roses and candy. It's a heady mixture of sweet and floral, and I bask in it for a long moment before she says, "You've always been—"

Her words taper off into heavy silence. It's always been like this with us, back and forth, tension and angst following us like a cloud, reminding us that we're supposed to be together.

But I always pushed her away. I made sure she never got too close. At least, that's what I tell myself. But there were times we did get close, and I almost lost control.

I set down my mug and take that last step toward her.

"Are you telling me every time he touches you, each time he kisses you and fucks your tight little cunt, you think of me?"

Another wince. She doesn't move when I reach up to grip her chin between my thumb and forefinger. When I force her eyes to land on mine, I see emotion dancing wildly like flames in a breeze.

"Yes." One word. The admission I'd been waiting for. It's barely a whisper, but I heard her. My cock thickens in my jeans, throbbing against my zipper. I want to be inside her so badly, my blood zings with lust.

"And when you come for him?" I challenge, pushing her to admit her feelings for me even though I shouldn't. But I do it because I want to hear the words fall from her lips. I need to listen to her voice, her desire for me.

"You're the only man I ever wanted," she confesses while I hold onto her. It's only a small connection, but it's weighty. I release her chin before sliding my hand to the back of her neck, and I pull her closer. "But I can't cheat," she throws out quickly as my lips brush along hers.

"You won't cheat on a bastard like him?" I taunt, a sly grin curling my lips at the soft gasp that tumbles from her mouth.

"As much as I want this," she tells me earnestly, her voice raw with emotion, "I'll not be the one in the wrong." Her palms land on my chest, the heat of her touch scorching me.

A split-second decision and I swipe my thumb along

her lips, the plump flesh under my touch sends raw desire through my veins. I'm close enough to take what I want. I could kiss her, even if she doesn't agree to it.

But I'm not a rogue.

And she means too much to me for me to force my hand.

"Then leave him," I finally murmur. It's almost a plea, and I'm certain she hears the imploring in my tone. "You know you don't belong to him. He's nothing more than a substitute for what you really want."

This time, I'm gifted with a smile, one that used to make my chest ache. For so long, I've allowed my anger to blind me to her. But right now, in this moment, we're Cass and Kaly from all those years ago. With no lies, no highs, and no fucking fiancés.

"There are things you don't know," she finally whispers. "I can't tell you, but you need to believe me; if I could walk away, I would." What she doesn't realize is I know all about what Paulo is doing, why she's with him. She also has no idea that I'm going to ensure he's out of the picture. Once my plans are in place, I'll do it.

"Then leave." My voice is firm, the order clear. I step away from her, the air suddenly free of her sweet scent. How I wish I could bottle her fragrance and smell it whenever I please. For now, I'll live without it. But my mind has been made up.

She's mine.

And I'm not letting her go without a fight.

"I'm not going to just walk away from you, Cass. I came here—" She shakes her head. "I just need you to know I—"

"I said leave." Schooling my features, I sip my coffee, arching a brow at her, which only makes her tip her chin toward me. Defiance shimmers in her eyes, but she doesn't sass me, she doesn't offer a retort. For now, she leaves, and my chest aches as I watch her walk out.

Hours later, as the sun sets, I glance up and stretch. I've not been focused on work all day because all I can think about is Kaly. I should be working on the figures for Thorne Industries, but each time I look at the screen, I pull up photos of Kalyn. Her career is doing well; she's the face of her own clothing line, along with movies that have sold out in box offices worldwide. However, there is still something niggling at me.

It's not anger, not anymore. No, there's more to her story than meets the eye. With Harris looking into why she's back, and researching the fiancé, I should be able to relax, but I can't.

An idea pops into my head, and I pick up the phone, hitting dial on my assistant's number before I can rethink this.

"Mr. Thorne, how can I help?"

I shouldn't do this. It's not my game to play, but there's only one way I'm going to get Kalyn alone. We need to talk.

The party wasn't the time or place to hash out the past, but the forest behind Thorne Manor is. "I need one red rose on my desk in the next hour."

"I... uhm... okay, I can do that." Confusion in her voice is clear, but I hang up because I don't need to explain myself. I'll have the burnt rose sent to Kaly, a sign that I want to talk, an invite for her to meet me, *or not*. It will ultimately be her choice, and there are no guarantees that she will come. But deep down, my intuition tells me she'll be there.

Kalyn

THE BEDROOM DOOR WHOOSHES OPEN AS I SET DOWN my makeup and glance at Paulo. He's leaning against the door frame, his arms folded, and the look on his face is nothing short of rage.

"What's wrong?" I push to my feet, wondering if I need to placate him or to run and hide. When he gets like this, there's no talking to him, but if I can say something to calm him down, then perhaps it will save me a world of hurt.

"This arrived for you," he sneers, unfolding his arms; I notice a box in his hand that has a black ribbon tied around it. The shimmery silk looks expensive, and when he hands me the box, I tug at the bow. Lifting the lid, I have a feeling

I know what I'll find, and just like I thought, lying on a soft satin interior is the burnt red rose.

The fragile bud looks like it's been incinerated, but strangely enough, it's still kept its shape. The stem is long, free from leaves, but there is a pattern of thorns that twist around the thin, blackened stalk.

"Who's sent you this, *darling*?"

There's no card, but I know exactly where this came from. However, I cannot tell Paulo, because he'll only lose his mind, and when he does that, I have no choice but to obey.

"I'm not sure," I lie, but I don't meet his eyes. This man has been around me for the better part of two years, and when I'm lying, it's as if he can sniff me out. He knows when I'm sad, happy, and when I'm telling him lies to hide something. I turn for my dresser, setting the box down gently, taking in the burnt invitation.

"If I find out you're lying to me, Kalyn," Paulo says from behind me, his large body looming over mine. The heat of his chest at my back, sending shockwaves of fear skittering down my spine, "You know it will be dangerous for you." The threat is clear.

Without another word, he steps away, leaving me shivering, as he shuts the bedroom door behind him. Alone again, I take a long, deep breath and stare down at the rose. Cassian wants to meet; perhaps he'll finally exact his revenge on me. I thought for sure he would've done something the night of the party, in front of everyone, including my fiancé, but then again, he never was one for public displays; he'd rather find his pleasure alone, in the dark.

And his gratification, this time, will be making me pay for what I did.

Paulo has held so many things over my head since we met. I was young, innocent, and stupid when I first walked into the studio to pose for him. And when he realized I was merely prey to his predatory gaze, he took advantage. I fell into the lifestyle of the rich and famous, partying every weekend, enjoying the life I'd been given. Little did I know it all came with a cost.

At least, I should have known.

But I lost myself in the drugs, and when Paulo realized he could easily sway me with a pill, a line of white, or a joint, he took control. After the first year, I was hooked, taking in the highs with the lows. That's when my father got sick, when I broke down once more, and Paulo was there to pick up the pieces.

At first, I thought he was my hero. The man who swooped in when I least expected and would make everything okay. Even after the previous year, I hoped for the best. But when Paulo's true colors shone through, when I saw the monster behind the handsome façade, I realized my mistake.

My life was filled with missteps as I tried to guide myself through the darkness that claimed me as its victim, and yet,

I still try to find the light. My biggest regret, my only regret, is hurting Cassian when he didn't deserve it. Tonight, I'll make it right; I'll give him anything he wants, just to ensure he can forgive me. He needs to move on, like I have, and live his life free of the past. But even as I think that, I know it's a lie. I haven't really moved on, I couldn't. And Cassian knows it.

Now all I need to do is figure out a way to get out of the house and not alert Paulo of where I'm going. An idea comes to mind, and I pick up my phone; there's only one girl I know in Thorne Haven, one who knows about the past, about all the bullshit that's gone on in this town—Genevieve.

If she can cover for me, perhaps I can see Cassian tonight. I'm not sure what he has in store for me, but whatever it is, I know I deserve it. After the third ring, I hear a voice I haven't heard in a long time.

"Hello?"

"Genevieve, hi, it's Kalyn Narro," I say, nerves eating away at me. We were in the same school. When I was younger, I was in her sister's class but never became close with either of them. They were merely my acquaintances rather than friends.

"Twice in one week," she whispers, "I didn't think you'd ever come back here. Not after what happened." That's one thing I was worried about, that Genevieve would know about what went down with Cassian. She was more than in love with Damien for a long time, and I've heard rumors about her and Finn, ones she's never denied.

"I was wondering if you could help me with something. You're the only person I know in town." I shut my eyes so tight I see stars behind my lids. She doesn't have to do this. We're not exactly friends. But there's no other way I can get out of this house tonight.

"And why would I do that?"

"I received a rose, a burnt rose," I tell her, the words falling from my lips in a breathy whoosh. My stomach twists as her gasp comes through the line. She knows what it means. The game we used to whisper about when we were at school is more than an urban legend. The Thorne brothers, and the Haven brothers, leave a burnt rose on your doorstep, or have it delivered because they're showing an interest. Once you receive one, you have to meet them in the woods behind Thorne Manor, and that's when the real games begin.

"Cassian," his name is whispered over the line, and I nod to myself. She knows everything about us. There's no hiding from the past anymore, and there is no denying that I *want* to see him, even though the ring on my finger hangs heavily with accusation.

My relationship with Paulo is as fake as most of the people I've met in my time in LA, but Cassian can't know that. At least, I pray he doesn't because his family has connections, and he could garner information anytime he needs it. All I can do is pray he hasn't figured it out so I can use it to my advantage when I see him tonight.

"What do you need?" Genevieve asks then, shocking me because I didn't expect her to even consider helping me.

"I need to see him, but I can't get out of the house with my fiancé here," I whisper, hoping Paulo isn't eavesdropping. "If I can tell him that I'm meeting you, he'll allow me to leave."

"That sounds an awful lot like abuse," she observes slowly. I don't respond, because I can't. She's right. But there's nothing I can do other than endure it. Paulo has a hold over me, more than the drugs and the addiction. He's the one who's got my family's lives in his hands, and that means more to me than my happiness.

"I have nobody else to turn to, not right now," I implore her, praying silently that she says yes, that she'll help me.

A long sigh from the other end of the line comes through loud and clear. She's not happy about me asking for her assistance. "Fine, but I want to see you," she finally says, and I let out the breath that I'd been holding. "We need to meet before you see him because there is something I need to say."

Nodding once more, I respond, "Sure. I'll meet you at the entrance to the forest, where we used to park for the parties." It will be strange going back there, but I need to do this.

"Six forty-five, don't be late. And Kalyn, I'm only doing this because he wants it," she informs me easily. She's never been one to bullshit or beat around the bush, so to speak.

"Okay." Knowing that if I'm going to be playing this game with Cassian, I need to be there at seven. It gives us fifteen minutes to hash out whatever it is she wants to say. "Thank you." My words might have been lost to nothing because when I realize the line is dead, I wonder if she even heard me.

At least she's agreed to help.

I glance once more at the rose, and my stomach flutters at the thought of seeing him again. The party was nothing short of magical, and even in those short moments with Cassian, anger dancing in his beautiful eyes, I could see he still wanted me. There was desire laced with rage in his words, and that gives me hope that someday, he'll forgive me for what I did.

Even though I am almost certain Cassian knows the truth, I must play the part of the dutiful fiancée. For now. Cassian doesn't need to know what Paulo's doing because I have a feeling that it won't go down well, even if Cassian still hates me. He will hurt Paulo, and it won't end with Cassian walking away without blood on his hands.

Cassian

"**A**RE YOU SURE THIS IS A GOOD IDEA?" FINN ASKS AS I shrug on my black hoodie.

Am I?

No.

But I need to do it.

I'm about to respond when his phone buzzes in his pocket, dragging my thoughts away from my answer and to his expression when he pulls the device out. He glances at me before answering the call; I know it's Harris. James emailed me an hour ago, confirming that Kalyn's father is ill, a life-threatening disease that he's getting treatment for. But the thing that doesn't make sense is that the figures don't add up; she doesn't seem to have the money to pay for it, even though her career looks like it's taking off.

The other note he made in the file he sent over was that the Narros are selling their house as well as any belongings they own in Thorne Haven, meaning they're leaving for good. The problem with that is, it makes no sense.

They were loaded.

I recall the moment they moved into town, flashy cars, expensive furniture, they even renovated the mansion somewhat, with a tennis court, personal spa, and state-of-the-art theatre. Something happened, and I need to find out what the fuck it is. And if Kalyn can't tell me anything tonight, I'll have the team on it the moment I get back from my meeting with her.

"Well now," Finn says, interrupting my thoughts, and I realize he's finished his call while I've been lost inside my mind again.

"What's Harris found?" I ask, knowing that's who he was talking to. I'm tense, my shoulders are bunched up, and my hands are fisted at my sides. Every muscle in my body is screaming for release, for some answers that will make sense of everything to me.

"It seems the cashflow from the sale of the house is going directly to Paulo Morales, the fiancé." Finn settles on the chair at my desk that overlooks the back garden. "Another interesting tidbit is that this asshole has been keeping

Kalyn *home* with him for the past two years. Her short stint in rehab was nothing more than a smokescreen, a lie told to the press to keep them from digging too deep."

"But that makes no sense. Why would she lie about going into rehab?" My mind works as I try to put the pieces of the puzzle together, but each time I try to fit my ideas into place, they don't feel right. I should've asked her the last time we were together, but the moment Kalyn stepped up to me, my mind blanked out. She's always done this to me. Made me feel things I wasn't prepared for.

"Well, this guy has been in her life for a couple of years, the parents seem to have accepted him, but from her phone records, she's not had any contact with anyone other than her folks, and him, for those two years he's been around." Finn leans back, resting his left ankle over his right knee, and laces his fingers behind his head. His dark brow lifts ever so slightly when he watches me make sense of what he's just said.

"You're trying to tell me he's keeping her as some sort of prisoner?" The incredulous tone of my voice is evidence enough that I'm holding onto my restraint by a thread. I'm ready to make this fucker pay, to hurt him in ways that will make his worst nightmares seem like childhood dreams.

"It seems his money is," Finn says before picking up his pinging cell phone and scrolling through what I can only assume is information he's just received. He turns the screen toward me, showing me the email from Harris. This Morales asshole is loaded, and it seems the Narros got into trouble when they left Thorne Haven. I have a feeling they were hoping Kalyn's career would help them out of it.

I do notice something of interest in the bank statements, stopping my scrolling and looking at my brother. "There are payments going out of his account to some hospital in Hollywood. Do you think he's paying for her father's treatments?"

"More than likely." Finn nods slowly. "Which means Kalyn probably agreed to marry this bastard because he's ensuring her dad is getting medical care."

"But that still doesn't explain the rehab lie," I tell my brother as the pieces fall into place. If she didn't get treatment for her addiction, it means she's still taking that shit. "Do you think he's—?"

"Force-feeding her drugs to keep her compliant?" Finn finishes my thought and nods in response. "I don't see why not. He seems to be controlling all of them. The mother works as an assistant at some film studio, which has the Morales name written all over the ownership documents," Finn continues as he takes the phone and taps the screen. "And..." he whispers, stopping at a particular spot on the document before handing me his phone.

I scan the words, but my vision blurs when I take in just what I'm reading. My blood turns to ice, but the rage burning in my gut feels as if a volcano is about to erupt. I've been angry at people before; I've even made sure those who crossed a Thorne paid. But this is something else. And when I get my hands on Paulo Morales, I'll ensure he never sees the light of day again.

I glance at Finn who's smirking because he knows what's running through my mind—vengeance. There are times it seems he can read my thoughts, and there's one thing I can depend on when it comes to my youngest brother, he's always up for a fight.

"When I get home from meeting with her," I start, handing Finn his cell phone before I crush it in my fist, "we make our plans." It's almost time for me to leave. Knowing she'll be there at seven has me anxious because I don't want to miss this chance to talk to her, to get everything out in the open, and hear her side of the story.

"I'll be here, ready and waiting," Finn informs me before pushing to his feet and heading for the door. "Let me know when you get back; I'll be in my room doing some more research."

For a few moments, after he walks out, I consider what I want to do to Kalyn's fake fiancé, because that's what he is. There's no way she can love this bastard. He's nothing more than a bully.

Grabbing my wallet, keys, and phone, I make my way out to the garage and slide into the driver's seat of my stormy gray SUV with blacked-out windows. I turn on the engine, and the speakers blare out one of my favorite songs. One that reminds me of a time when things were less complicated, and all I wanted to do was claim Kalyn. "Peace of Mind" by Villain of the Story fills the car as I make my way to meet the girl I've wanted since I first laid eyes on her.

She's been through hell.

She's been alone through all this.

I haven't yet forgiven her for what she did to me, but I'm nowhere near as cruel as this motherfucking Paulo Morales is. I wanted to make her pay, to ensure she leaves Thorne Haven and never returns, but that was all my smokescreen. As I pull up to the entrance of our old party spot, I realize that what I really wanted was Kalyn in my arms, screaming my name as I finally claim what has always been mine—her.

I don't see anyone from the window, but before I get out and make my way to the spot, I know she'll be waiting. I inhale a couple of deep breaths, hoping they'll calm me down. But knowing what I do about her life, what she's been doing since she left Thorne Haven, I can't find it in myself to keep calm.

She made mistakes.

We all do.

Yes, the lie she told was harsh, but she'll most certainly pay for it once I've freed her from Paulo and chained her to me forever. The thought of keeping her as mine has been solidified in my thoughts. There's no going back. I can't. With that in mind, I pull out my phone and tap out a text to Dad.

Even though he doesn't know what's going on, asking him for help will ensure I can do what needs to be done tonight. I don't have to wait long for his response, and I'm surprised because usually around this time, he and his new wife are locked in their wing of the manor, not to be seen till morning.

Thankfully, he's agreed.

Slipping my phone back into my pocket, I push open the car door and inhale the woodsy scent of the forest. This is the place where I've lost myself so many times, I've lost count. It's dark already, and a chill has set in the air, which means it's time to have some fun with Kalyn. I hope she remembers the game.

I cup my hands at my mouth and offer up the cry of the game, two long whistles which echo amongst the thick tree trunks. And that's when my feet carry me into the shadows.

I'm coming for you, little liar.

Kalyn

THE ECHO OF HIS CALL HAS ME JUMPING IN SHOCK, MY feet moving on instinct through the trees. I don't run because I don't want to; I don't need to because I know Cassian will eventually find me. Instead, I make my way toward the lake, slipping behind the thick trunks every now and then, hoping he won't get to me before I reach the water.

My talk with Genevieve didn't go as expected. She knows more than she should about what Paulo is like, and I didn't expect it. Her guess about his demeanor was perfectly on point. And the fact that she knows about our relationship, the possessiveness of my fiancé doesn't sit well with me.

Guilt had eaten at me as she tried to warn me to seek help, but what she doesn't realize is if I do anything to anger him, my father will be left with no medical treatment, and it's expensive. More than we can afford.

Anger takes hold of me when I think about how Dad had squandered our money as if he had a never-ending supply. And his choices have brought me to this moment, where we're going to have to sell off everything to pay back what we owe Paulo. But not only that, I'm indebted to a man I hate. On the one hand, I blame my dad, and on the other, I blame myself for agreeing to go ahead with it.

Shaking my head of the errant thoughts, I focus on my steps and finally make it to the clearing where the full moon is shimmering on the glassy lake. Silver glints at me seconds before a hand slips over my mouth, causing a scream to muffle against the soft, warm palm that's covering my lips. His other arm snakes around my waist, and he pulls me against his hard, toned body.

"Got you, little liar," Cassian's whisper skitters over my cheek, causing goosebumps to rise in its wake. "I'm going to release you," he tells me, and I can feel the smile on his expression as he presses his lips to my ear. "No screaming."

Slowly, he removes himself from holding me, and I immediately miss his touch. But I know he didn't bring me here to reminisce about old times; this is for him to extract his payback.

I spin on my heel the moment I'm free, coming face-to-face with his beautiful eyes, shadowed under the black hoodie he's wearing. He's clean-shaven, his smooth, angular jaw greeting me as I take him in. Full lips curl into a sinister smirk that makes my stomach tumble with nerves.

"I didn't think you'd come," he finally says, pushing the hood off, and I notice his hair is shorter than usual. The buzzcut suits him. My fingertips tingle to feel his soft hair, to run my fingers over his head while he's feasting on me.

"Neither did I." Flicking my gaze to the ground to clear my wayward thoughts, I focus on his feet, hidden in black combat boots. Cassian looks like the epitome of dark and dangerous as he leans back against a tree. He crosses his arms in front of his broad chest, and I can only imagine the muscles bunching under the heavy material of his clothes.

"Where's the unlucky fiancé?" he questions; the angry bite to his words isn't lost on me. Snapping my gaze to his, I take note of the jealousy that's turned his lips downward at the corners; the blaze in his eyes doesn't hide his emotions. One thing I recall about Cassian, even from all those years ago, he could never hide his feelings from me. His eyes were always so expressive. I could tell when he was angry, happy, and even turned on.

My cheeks heat at the memories. I need to focus, but with him looking so good, bringing back feelings I've long since buried, it's difficult to think straight.

"What do you want from me, Cassian?" I ask softly instead of answering his question. "I can't be out here too long. There are things you don't know—"

"About the bastard you agreed to marry?" he challenges before pushing away from the tree. He stalks toward me, causing me to stumble backward. Thankfully I'm wearing trainers and find my footing on the uneven ground. "About why you're really here?" he asks a different question this time, and even though my mouth opens, I can't find words to answer him.

Does he know?

He can't. There's no way he could've found out about anything that has happened in the past few years, especially the last two.

"Tell me, little liar," Cassian taunts, "does he make you feel like I used to?" This time, his question heats my whole body, from head to toe, and it feels as if I'm burning up from a fever. He continues stalking toward me, forcing me back against one of the thick trunks, and soon, I'm pinned between him and the tree, with no escape in sight.

Cassian leans in, his mouth at my ear in an instant. His warm breath fans over me, sending shockwaves of need coursing through me. I can't answer him because he already knows the truth. No man has ever made me feel what he does.

Shame fills me at the reminder. Because I can't have

Cassian, he never wanted me, not then, and certainly not now. He's only toying with me tonight to get his vengeance.

"Does he make your pretty pussy wet?" he whispers, causing a gasp of shock to tumble from my lips. "Because I doubt that he could make your body react like this." His teasing continues when he trails his knuckles over my cheek, down my neck, to the neckline of my T-shirt. He tugs on it gently before running his fingertips up my collarbone to my throat, where he wraps his hand firmly around the slender column. "Does he know how you used to chase me around like a puppy dog? Needing my attention only on you. And does he know you used to touch your cunt at night thinking about me defiling you every which way?" His words are filthy, harsh, but they're also true.

My cheeks are burning from embarrassment as a whimper of need escapes my lips. Cassian chuckles, but his hold on my throat tightens when he pushes back to lock his heated gaze on mine. There's no hate in his stare, only raw desire.

"W-what d-d-do you w-want, Cassian?" I finally manage to whisper. I'm not scared, and he knows it because he tips his head to the side, his eyes narrowing as he regards me with interest.

"I want the truth, Kaly," he responds in a voice so low, so dangerous, I struggle to swallow the lump of fear that suddenly fills my throat. "I want the honest, brutal truth from you because I'm sick of lies and stories."

Suddenly, he releases me, pushing away from me as if I've burned him. But he doesn't look away. He keeps those teal orbs pinned on me as if he'll be able to dig out the truth from me with a glare.

Perhaps he can because I find myself aching to confess, to tell him about my life, about Paulo. I want to ask him for help, but I doubt he could ever give that to me. I doubt he'd even want to.

"Why?" I ask instead. "Why do you want to know about me?"

He regards me for a long while before responding, "Because it would make it easier for me to break you." And that sinister grin is back on his face. The way his full, pink lips curl, even in this darkness, makes me want to feel them on every part of me. What Cassian doesn't realize, though, is that I've been broken long before he came along.

"I'm getting married to the man I love," I lie, praying with all I have that he doesn't see through me. That he doesn't see the truth in my bitter words.

He laughs; it's a deep chuckle that confirms he doesn't believe a word I'm saying. "Do you truly think I'm going to believe that?"

"You have a high regard for yourself, Cassian Thorne. I didn't sit around and wait for you to come and save me," I bite out, the anger at how he used to push me away just because he declared me too young for him takes hold. Granted, I was sixteen, and I knew he would get into trouble if we took it a step too far, but I was all grown-up, I could choose what I wanted, and I ached for him.

But he never lost control.

Until now.

"You see," Cassian says, dragging me out of the thoughts racing through my mind, bringing me back to the present. "I thought that's what was happening. You had moved on to something *better*. I figured you were all grown-up and ready to take on the world," he announces with a flourish. "But then I had my men look into this little charade you're playing."

He stops moving and just stares at me. The truth in his gaze burns right through me. *He knows.* I don't know what he's found out, but he knows something more is going on between Paulo and me; that much is clear.

"What do you mean?" I cross my arms over my chest, needing to hold myself together. Cassian cannot know about what happened to me. He couldn't have learned about Paulo's hold over me. In the silence of the night, I pray he doesn't know everything.

But when he steps closer to me, there's a glint of rage in his eyes that wasn't there earlier. And in that moment, I realize Cassian knows everything. I want to break down, to fall to my knees and cry, but I swallow back the pain, the heartbreak taking hold of me, and I focus on keeping my tears at bay.

"You're not going back to that house tonight," Cassian declares, causing my attention to snap to his. "I'm not allowing you to spend another night in a house with that bastard. And if he wants a fight, I'm ready for him."

"I don't understand," I whisper hoarsely, my voice cracking with emotion. "If I don't go back, if I anger him, he'll stop paying—"

"For your father's treatment," Cassian finishes my sentence. "I know what he's doing, and I've already taken care of it."

My mouth pops open in shock. "What?" The word comes out as a squeak of surprise. That is most definitely not what I expected him to say.

"I'm not letting you go near him again, Kalyn. If anyone is going to hurt you and make you cry, it will be me, and trust me when I say that when I do, it will not be from pain, but from pleasure."

"Cassian, you're not making sense. You cannot keep me hostage here," I answer, but my head is spinning with confusion. The man in front of me hates me, with good reason. He shouldn't be stepping into my life as a hero because I don't need that. All I wanted was forgiveness.

He steps up to me once more, closing the distance between us. Our bodies flush as he captures my chin between his finger and thumb. "I've been angry at you for a long time, Kaly," he tells me earnestly, his eyes shimmering as he looks into mine. "I've spent my life wanting revenge, to make you pay for your lie, for telling your parents I would ever get you into this sick addiction of yours."

"When your father spoke to them, told them the truth, they—"

"I know they believed him," he interrupts me. "But it was your lie that sparked my anger. That you could even say something like that about me, that's what shattered me, little liar."

"I'm sorry, Cassian, I truly am." This time, my voice breaks, and the tears I'd been keeping at bay slip from my lashes and trickle down my cheeks. A smile dances on Cassian's mouth as he takes in my broken expression. I know he'll enjoy my tears because he's spent years wanting to cause them, wanting to make me beg and cry.

"Oh, you will be," he warns. "But as I said, you're not going back to that bastard." He pulls me closer by my chin, so there's nowhere else to go. Our mouths are a hairsbreadth away, and his warmth consumes me as he whispers along my lips, "You're mine now, and I'm not letting you out of my sight until I've extracted my pound of flesh. Once you're paid up, you'll be begging me to keep you, just like you did all those years ago."

"I don't understand." My words come out as a breathy

whisper, one that I admonish myself for because I don't want Cassian to know just how much his words have affected me.

"You'll live at Thorne Manor until the Narro house is sold. While you're at the manor, you'll pay me back for that lie, for those words that fell from your lips."

"How?" I mumble, inhaling his breath and allowing him to steal mine. His lips touch mine, it's featherlight, but enough to cause my thighs to squeeze together.

A flicker of warning dances in those pretty eyes. I should ask him why he wants me to stay at the manor, why he wants to keep me from Paulo, but all I can think about right now is kissing him. And wanting him to finally claim me as his.

But he pushes away and says, "You'll soon learn. Come." Cassian spins on his heel, leaving me heaving breaths to keep from passing out. His scent is all over me; the cedar and mint of his cologne have engulfed me, and as I rush to follow him through the trees, it's the only thing I can smell.

I don't know what he has in store for me, but I have a feeling his revenge will be nothing compared to what Paulo's put me through. So, before I have time to rethink my actions, I slip into the passenger seat of the SUV and watch as Cassian joins me.

"What about my father? Paulo's paying for his treatment."

Cassian glances over at me, his right hand gripping the steering wheel while his left elbow leans against the door.

He looks like the ultimate bad boy as he grins. "Don't you worry your pretty head about that," he tells me. "Your father is being taken care of by Thorne Industries."

"I still don't understand," I say, imploring him with my gaze to tell me the whole story. "What about my car?"

"Don't worry about that either," he informs me. "I'll have one of my men bring it to the house." Cassian starts the engine, a song blares through the speakers cutting off any more conversation we could have. Instead of forcing him to talk, I settle in for the short ride back to the manor and pray that whatever his plan is, my family is safe.

Cassian

HER SCENT IS ALL OVER ME.
Even as I attempt to focus, all I can think about is just how close I was to her, so close I almost stole a kiss when her lips brushed against mine. I almost took her right there against the tree. It would've been a release I have craved for years, but I needed to clear my head. I needed to think about this logically because her penance will have to be deserving of her crime.

When I finally kill the engine, the silence that hangs in the air is thick with tension. I should say something. Perhaps I should tell her that I'm doing this to get her away from an abusive bastard, but I want to hurt her as well. Not like he did, I just want her to know that no matter where she goes in life, she's mine, she always will be.

Nobody can make her feel like I do.

No other man, or woman, can make her want, desire, and yearn for them like she does for me.

"I don't know what to say to you anymore," Kalyn whispers, her hands twisted together. "Why are you bringing me here?"

I ponder her words, her question, for a long while before I glance at her. "I may want you to pay for what you did, but I'm no monster. That bastard..." I allow my words to filter into nothing because anything I say will have the rage boiling up inside me again. And the last thing I need right now is to get into a fight with him.

When I take him down, it will be with precision, with class, and I'll make sure he never has access to vulnerable young women again. I've seen men like him, time and again, and they always get what's coming to them.

"What will your family say if I'm here?" Kaly asks, dragging my attention back to her. I focus on her pretty face. She's thinner than she was at school. But her beauty still remains perfectly in place. High cheekbones, full, plump lips that just beg to be claimed, almond-shaped eyes, and straight, button nose. She is every photographer's dream. Her wild, curly brown hair has highlights of gold in strands that only add to her unique beauty.

"My father doesn't mind," I tell her before turning my attention to the front of the car. I've parked just outside the garage door, and I allow my focus to remain on the wall instead of Kaly. "My brother, on the other hand, he's about as angry as I am."

Honesty was what I always gave her. Even when we were still at school, even when I knew the truth would hurt, I would offer it up as a gift. She did the same for me, and that's how our friendship bloomed, like a rose. The sweet bud of new possibilities blossomed until she lied. That's when the petals fell, and the happiness I once knew came crashing down.

"I didn't mean to hurt you," she finally says. Her hands shake as she reaches for me, and I wonder if she's going through withdrawals or if she's nervous to touch me. When her fingertips land on my arm, sparks shoot through me like they always have when we made contact.

Her heat is my drug.

Her touch is my addiction.

Being with her is a high so sweet, I never want to come down.

"What you didn't *mean* to do and what you *did* do are two very different things, little liar," I tell her before pushing open the car door. "Now come with me; it's time to get some rest." The moment I get out of the vehicle, fresh air hits me, and I miss her fragrance. It's always been like this with us; each time I would leave her, I'd miss her.

It's stupid to be so emotional over one person, but then I see how Damien is with Nesrin, and it all makes sense. I fell in love with Kalyn a long time ago; I just didn't want to admit it. To her, or to myself.

Perhaps that's why she did what she did. Maybe she thought if she were to hurt me, it would make it easier to leave. Whatever her reasons for lying, it doesn't matter now because I finally have her where I want her—under my roof.

I lead her inside, and the moment we walk into the kitchen, I'm met with Finn, who's working on his laptop at the table. His gaze flicks to me, then lands on the woman behind me. I notice his brow arching in question, but I don't offer an answer.

This wasn't part of our plan. I was meant to send her back to Paulo, but when I looked at her tonight, saw how she reacted to me, I knew there was no love between them. There's nothing more than his hold over her, and I intend to break it.

"Kalyn," Finn greets as he shuts his laptop, twisting in his chair to get a better look, I'm guessing. "It's nice to see you again. Didn't expect you to be here," he says, his words filled with questions as he glances between her and me.

"I-I didn't expect to be here," she murmurs, standing

awkwardly in the middle of the room, her hands twisting in front of her, and the thought I had in the car returns. *Is she going through withdrawals?* "Cassian said I was going to stay here for a bit."

"I see," Finn responds as I grab a couple of bottles of water from the fridge before handing one to Kalyn. Her hands are shaking as she takes the bottle from me, her eyes wide as they land on mine when she sees that I notice her problem.

I gesture to her, taking in the way she's trembling like a fucking leaf. "Has he been doing this to you?" I ask, gritting my teeth as I wait for the answer, but even as I ask her, I know what the response will be, and that does nothing to calm my anger.

"I... He doesn't do it all the time. I mean, when he's angry, or if he needs me to listen," she informs Finn and me in a hushed whisper. Her cheeks turn bright red as she confesses, and shame flickers in her eyes when she looks at me. "I-I find it difficult to say no, to fight it."

"How did he find you?" I ask, my hand gripping the water bottle so hard, I expect it to shatter any moment. "How did he know that you were in such dire straits?"

"We met at a party; it was after the release of my first movie," Kalyn says as I guide her to a chair. She settles in, opposite Finn, beside me. Once again, the scent of her perfume assaults my senses, but I keep my focus on her words. "He was charming, asked me out, and I said yes. It was so lonely in Hollywood with Dad working and my mother at her job, which seemed to always keep her busy."

"And the parties he took you to, were they all at a certain club or someone's house?" This comes from Finn as he opens his laptop once more. There's something about my brother that I've always admired; he loves a good mystery. And he's probably got ideas of Paulo's reasons for ensuring Kalyn was under his control.

"Well…" she ponders this for a moment before nodding, "yes, he has a few clubs in town that he used to frequent, and I'd be with him. Other times, it would be one of his homes—he had three—which we would end up at."

"And you never remembered the night before when you woke the next morning," Finn says. It's not a question because he's nodding, sure of himself; he's clearly figured out Paulo's plan.

"N-no," Kalyn says, "I would always wake up with a hangover, and I thought perhaps it was the shots from the night before, or…" Her voice cracks, and silence surrounds us, but Finn's tapping on the keyboard confirms my brother is already working out how we can get our vengeance for Kaly.

He finally stops typing, then spins the computer around to face us. "Were these the clubs and houses you were in?"

There are photos on the screen of some exclusive-looking places. The houses are huge. People filling up the space, all dressed in the finest designer brands and holding glasses of alcohol. I don't doubt these were raucous, but what bothers me is that in each of the photos, there are men dressed in all black, as if they're security.

Most times I've been to parties with celebrities, the bodyguards would spend their time outside. None of them were ever indoors. The reasoning was that if there was something to use as blackmail, it wouldn't be seen by the *staff*.

"Yes," Kaly whispers before taking a sip of the chilled water. "I remember a few of those. I just don't know what happened. I recall arriving; all the guests would flock around us, mostly talking to Paulo. But after a few minutes of being there, my brain would go fuzzy, and I would wake up in bed."

There's one question I want to ask, I need to ask, but I know the answer will ensure I'll be flying into a fit of rage and racing out the door to kill the fucker. But Kaly has to tell us.

"Were you ever in pain the next morning? Not a hangover, but physically," I hiss, my hands fisting on the table, nails digging into my palms to attempt to appear calm when I'm anything but. "Was there ever any indication you were involved in…" I can't finish the sentence because I know if I do, I'll lose it.

"I-I…" For a long moment, all I hear is silence; it's deafening. Kalyn's focus is on the water bottle, her shaking fingers tugging at the label.

I'm so tense, my shoulders ache from being bunched up, and my arms are shaking from trying to rein in my anger. I could so easily kill.

"There were a few times I thought we'd done things the night before. He wasn't always rough, or violent, but I knew something very bad had happened." Her confession has me shooting to my feet. Finn is quick to react to me, his hand on my shoulder, gripping me so tight it hurts as his fingers dig into my muscle in warning. Then Kalyn whispers, "I'm sorry."

The moment those two words hit my ears, I shrug my brother off and spin toward Kalyn, whose eyes are wide with shock when my palms hit the table. I lean in, getting my face right in front of hers. We're inches apart, and what I see in those pretty almond-shaped orbs is fear. She's scared of me. I would be too. But not for her safety, for that bastard who hurt her.

"Don't you ever apologize for what you went through." My words are filled with rage and venom. The violence that's shooting through every nerve ending in my body twists around my lungs, squeezing the air from me. I'm ready for war with this bastard. "I have to know what happened to you, Kaly."

"Cass," Finn's calm voice breaks through the cloud of pure forcefulness that's surrounding me, and I push away from Kalyn. "Can you tell us?" He focuses on Kaly, and after a while, she nods.

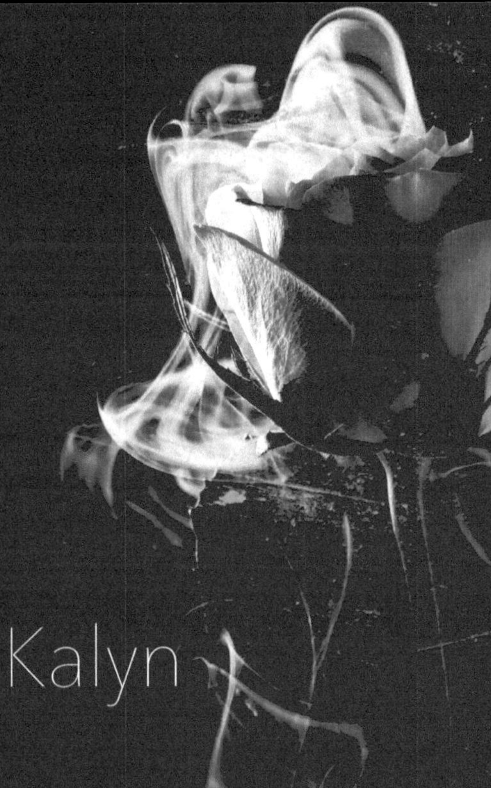

Kalyn

I HAVEN'T SPOKEN ABOUT THIS TO ANYONE. NOT EVEN a therapist. The fear of being judged, of having people know I've done something bad, made me want to hide away from the truth. But with Cassian and Finn, there is no hiding anymore.

Maybe, just maybe, they can help me.

"Eight months ago, I was in a very low place. Work had been so busy, I hadn't had time to spend with my folks, and my dad was getting worse. The cancer had spread. But then, something happened," I finally start, my voice is merely a whisper, but both men are now seated across from me, watching me intently. I don't look at them because if I do,

I'll break down, and I won't be able to confess my darkest secret.

"I wanted to go to an after-party to meet with a director, but I'd been feeling sick for a few weeks. I didn't think anything of it," I say while trying to keep my voice even, to keep the words from halting due to fear. "It was a busy time for me with both movies hitting the big screen. Paulo was there every single day, watching me. It felt like I was under more scrutiny, more than the paparazzi ever exhibited.

"Where were you staying at the time?" Finn asks, causing me to finally look up at both men. Cassian looks like he's barely holding onto his sanity at this point, so I focus on Finn.

"One of Paulo's houses. He kept me there, night and day. If I was in the studio, on location or had an appearance, he'd take me, wait until I was done, and then drive me back to the house."

"Where were your folks?" Again, it's Finn who asks this, and Cassian sits silently, his teal eyes turning dark with anger at every word I utter.

"Dad was already in the hospital, and Mom was working night and day at the studio," I tell them. "I was alone. And I thought Paulo cared, ensuring I got to work when I needed to be. It was..."

"Nice?" Cassian sneers; his hands are twisted on the table as he leans forward. "He was being *nice?*" I know he's not angry at me because he would've said something to taunt me if he was. He's angry at how Paulo twisted my perception of him, ensuring I was leaning on and relying on him for everything.

"Yeah," I admit. "When I started getting sick, he took me to a doctor to get tests done, but now that I recall, the doctor didn't say anything was the matter. But Paulo met with him alone, after I was done. They were in the office for a long while, and when Paulo took me home, he seemed agitated. I don't remember much more of that day or the night."

Cassian is on his feet, pacing back and forth as he tugs off his hoodie, and I get a glimpse of the man under the material. His shoulders are broad, muscled. He's filled out so much from the boy I once knew. Veins line his arms, pulsing as he fists and releases his hands at his sides.

His torso is lean, but he's sculpted; the way his body is tapered from his broad chest to his narrow waist makes my mouth water. The black jeans he's wearing hug his muscled thighs. Everything about him is built for the hunt, a predator, ready to pounce on his prey.

When he finally stops pacing, those teal eyes, now dark as the ocean, pin me to the spot, and my breath catches in my throat. "What happened after that?" His voice is menacing, drenched with something dark, something dangerous, and it makes me shiver. I'm not afraid of Cassian hurting me; I'm scared that he's going to do something he can never come back from. I'm terrified he'll kill Paulo.

There are choices you make, things you do in life. You act out, and you don't think of the consequences, the aftermath. And I pray with all I have that Cassian doesn't do something stupid that will forever change his life. Not for me.

"I-I think that's enough," I whisper.

"Tell me what the fuck happened!" His voice booms across the room, and I expect the windows to shatter from the pure force of it. His hands slam down on the wooden surface, causing me to jump in shock. I've seen Cassian in every mood imaginable, but I've never seen him so filled with rage before.

"Hey, man," Finn tries to placate his brother. "We know what—"

"Shut the fuck up, Finn," Cassian throws back over his shoulder to his brother. "I want her to tell me. I want to hear the words uttered because when I take action, I want the reminder of this pretty little liar's confession to be my fuel."

He turns his attention on me once more, and then I see it. It's only a flicker of emotion, but I read it in those eyes. He cares for me. It may not be love, but there's something there, and if he cares, perhaps he'll listen to me. Maybe he'll hear me out and not do something stupid.

"I-I..." My voice cracks as agony shoots through my chest at the memory. At how callously Paulo had acted when I was admitted to the hospital. Tears burn my eyes, they linger on my lashes, and when I blink, they trickle down my cheeks.

I expect Cassian to laugh, to say something taunting to me. I am certain he's enjoying my pain, but when he speaks, my heart catapults into my throat.

"I'm going to kill him." There is no messing around, no humor in his tone, and it's evident that he's most certainly going to do as he says. "Tell me, Kalyn, you need to talk about it," he says gently as he settles into the chair beside me.

His arm wraps around my shoulders as he pulls me closer to his body. I nestle in the crook of his hold, and his strong, firm touch calms me somewhat as he leans in to meet my gaze.

"I need you to say it," he whispers. "You have to recognize what you've been through." I don't know why he's doing this; it doesn't matter if I say it or not; the truth is, I lost so much, and he has no reason to help me.

"I-I m-miscarried." More tears fall, burning tracks down my cheeks as I recall the agony. The blood. The pain that I can never hide from. As much as he wanted to make me forget by getting me high every day, keeping me in a fog of whatever he would give me, I remember. Every minute of that drive to the hospital, when two of Paulo's friends, who are doctors, took me into a private room. Where they administered medication, put me on pain killers that made me lose consciousness. I spent weeks with my head in the clouds.

"Kalyn." Cassian's voice breaks through the memories assaulting me, and I glance up to find his teal eyes shimmering as he regards me. "Nobody should go through that alone." His voice, tender and warm, wraps itself around me, and for a long moment, I bask in his affection.

Swallowing past the lump in my throat, I whisper, "H-h-he didn't care. He watched me b-b-bleed," I choke out the words as pain lances my chest at the memory. "At first I wasn't sure what was going on, my mind was fuzzy, but..."

"My sweet girl," Cass coos as he watches me, waiting for the moment I've expelled every hurtful recollection. With what Paulo did to me, I could be here all day confessing.

"It was only days later that I remembered what happened, how I had come to lose..." I blink and tears tumble freely. "He and two of his friends, the doctors who treated me after, they..."

Silence hangs heavily as I try to find the words. I want to tell them, tell Cassian, but as my salty emotion burns tracks down my cheeks, I suddenly feel weak.

"Kalyn, you don't have to—"

Cassian's voice is tight with feral rage, so I interrupt and murmur the last part of my pain, "They gave me drugs that would bring about the loss. From what I remember, Paulo talking to them about not wanting children and... one of the doctors said he knew how to remove it with a mix of pills."

A whispered *fucking hell* comes from Finn who's voice is tinged with wrath. Cassian cups my cheek, but the anger causes his hands to tremble against me. His eyes burning with vengeance and heartbreak as his thumb swipes over the tears that collect on the pad. He mimics the motion on the other cheek and locks his gaze on mine.

But before he can say anything more, I whisper, "I felt nothing. I was numb for so long." The plea in my tone is unmistakable. I want help. I want Cassian. But I'll never be whole. At least, that's one thing I'm certain of as he takes my hand and brings it to his lips.

"I'm going to make him pay, over and over again." The promise is filled with conviction, and I don't doubt him and then he pulls my face to his, our lips fusing with regret and pain.

The softness of his kiss cracks my heart further, and I wonder how he can still be sitting here after knowing everything about me. My life has been a series of mistakes that I can't come back from.

"Come with me," Cassian says before taking my hand as he rises from the chair. He pulls me up, and I have no choice but to follow. "I'll see you in the morning; we'll talk about the plan." He glances over his shoulder at Finn, who's watching us intently, and my cheeks heat at the way his lips curve into a grin.

"Oh, I'll be waiting, brother," Finn says. "Goodnight,

Kalyn." He offers a mock salute as we walk out of the kitchen and make our way through the house.

It's enormous. And with every step on the expensive tiles, I wonder when my phone is going to ring. Paulo thinks I'm with Genevieve, but it won't be long before he's looking for me because I haven't returned.

I need to tell Cassian, but he seems to be on a mission to get wherever we're going. Down the long hallway on the ground floor, he leads me all the way to the back of the house until we get to the end, where two doors are waiting for us. Both are shut.

Cassian takes a key from his pocket and unlocks one before pushing it open and allowing me to step through first. Inside, I find a double bed that is covered in soft green bedding. The windows are shut, but there's an icy chill in the air. The curtains are white, with small green flowers on them, offering a brightness to the room even though the overhead light is fairly dim.

"This is where you'll sleep tonight," Cassian says from behind me, causing me to spin on my heel. I'm exhausted. Emotionally, physically, and mentally. It's been a while since I forced myself to think about the baby. Even though it was early in the pregnancy, I still feel this emptiness that shouldn't be there.

"He's going to call," I tell Cassian. "He won't stop until he's found me. He thinks I'm with Genevieve. It was the only way I could get out of the house without him following."

Cassian nods. "Give me your phone." It's an order, one that I accept and obey immediately as I hand over the device. It's not locked. It's never been because that way, Paulo can see who I've been contacting.

All this time, I've been stuck in this abusive circle, and I didn't even think to get out. That's not true, I have wondered what it would be like to be free, but with my father's treatment at the forefront of my mind, I didn't think I had a choice.

"Why are you helping me?" I ask Cassian as he taps out something on my phone. I should look to see what he's doing, but I'm too tired to fight any more tonight. I've been tired for a long time, but with the drugs that have kept me going, it didn't fully hit me until now.

My hands are still trembling as I stand and watch Cassian. The silver chain that hangs around his neck is so familiar, and I focus on it, trying to recall where it's from.

But when he lifts his gaze to mine, all thoughts in my mind wash away. He stalks toward me, stopping inches from me. The warmth of his cedar cologne engulfs me, consuming my worries and calming me.

"Because no matter what, I'll always be your rock," he affirms before tugging my chin between his thumb and forefinger. His lips brush along mine, and the heat of his breath wafts over me, taking me prisoner.

"I thought you wanted to see me pay for what I did?" I don't know why I'm challenging him like this, poking the bear while it's asleep, but I can't help myself. It's how we've always been—me, a sassy little shit, and him, a demanding bastard.

"I do." His whisper feathers along my lips. "And I'll make you pay, on my terms," he tells me, and I don't doubt for a moment that he's telling the truth. "You need sleep. I've handled your *fiancé* for tonight," he spits the word as if it's poison on his tongue. "I'll be back in the morning to bring you breakfast."

Suddenly, he releases me, pushing away from me as if I've burned him. A shiver wracks through me when I realize he's about to lock me in this room.

"Cassian, please don't—"

"There's water in the fridge," he says as he points to a small under-counter cooler. "And the bathroom is through that door." I take in where he's gesturing. "Don't try anything stupid because I'll know." And then he's gone.

Racing to the door, I bang on the wooden surface, and I wonder if he's standing on the other side listening to me beg. My mind is whirling with thoughts, fears, questions. My hands are shaking even more now than they were earlier.

The room is comfortable with the enormous bed I'm currently lying on. In my attempt to calm my erratic heartbeat, I focus on my surroundings and take in the off-white curtains and the mirror that sits across the windows.

It's a lovely bedroom, and I wish I could truly enjoy the space, but my mind is racing. The sky outside is black with no moon or stars in sight. I should get up and close the drapes, but my legs are trembling.

Closing my eyes, I breathe deeply, fisting my hands and unclenching them. "I'm okay. I can do this. Cassian is going to help me." My stomach twists as anxiety takes hold, and the need for something to ease my nervous energy is at the forefront of my mind.

Usually, this is the time Paulo would give me something to calm me down, to allow me to sleep peacefully. But tonight, I'm going cold turkey, and I'm not sure I'll survive the night.

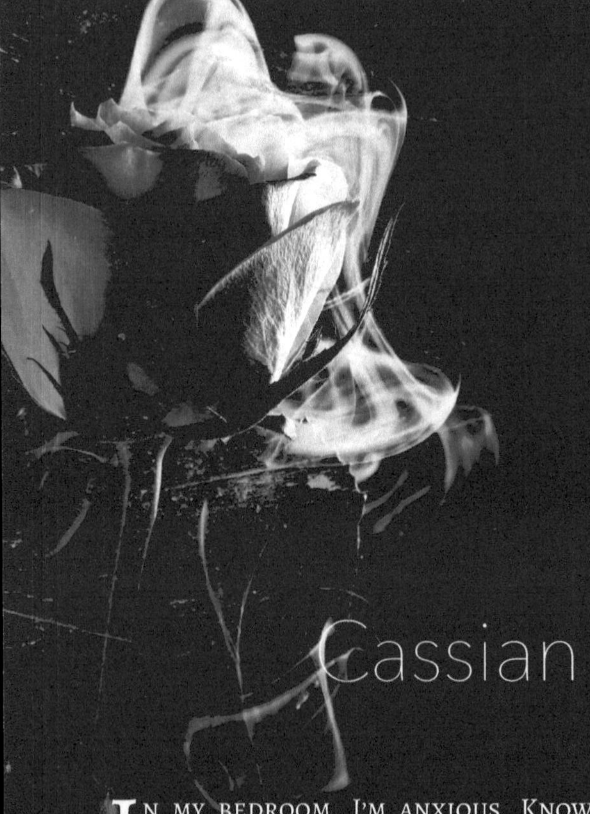

Cassian

I N MY BEDROOM, I'M ANXIOUS. KNOWING SHE'S ONLY downstairs, locked up tight, has me aching to go to her, to heal the pain I saw so clearly in her eyes. But if I did that, I wouldn't be able to stop until she was nothing more than a whimpering mess. And her coming off whatever the fuck Paulo got her addicted to isn't going to be easy for her.

Pulling out my phone, I hit call on Ulrich's number. The doctor I've known all my life has always been a help when needed, and this time, he's going to have to be here for my girl.

"Mr. Thorne," he greets, his voice happy and light.

"Doctor, I need your help. I'm sorry it's so late, but I have my girlfriend here and she's been struggling with addiction. I don't want to send her to the hospital just yet. Would you be able to come and check in on her?"

"How long has this been going on?" I can hear the worry in his tone.

Sighing, I tell him the story, how Kalyn is only now coming to terms with what's been going on, the abuse, the addiction. And even though she hasn't asked for help yet, I need him to make sure she gets through this.

"Give me thirty minutes and I'll be there, I'm just finishing up at the hospital. In the mean time, stay with her, try to keep her calm and don't let her out of your sight."

"See you soon." I hang up before shoving my phone into my pocket. I could taunt her until she focuses on me only. I could take her to the edge, leaving her teetering, needing nothing more than orgasm after orgasm that I'll bestow on her beautiful body. But that's not how I want to help her. Because turning her addiction from drugs to sex is unhealthy, no matter how much I crave a taste of her.

My bedroom door opens, and I know it's Finn. I don't look away from the garden, my focus on the window in front of me that offers a view of the woods that line the back of our property.

"I have a feeling someone's gotten way under your skin," Finn remarks from behind me. I'm not sure how to answer him because I know Kalyn has always been under my skin.

She burrowed herself there long before I even realized what had happened.

I spent my youth enjoying the single life. I never once had a girlfriend, and even when I thought about a relationship, the only person who ever crossed my mind was her.

"There's nothing to talk about," I tell Finn, and the lie tastes bitter on my tongue. We've always been close. There's nothing my brother doesn't know about me. And I know it's the same the other way around. But with her, I want to keep her all to myself. "Have we found a weakness in that bastard's armor?" I ask instead before he has time to talk about Kalyn.

Finn sighs. "Yeah," he tells me, causing me to turn around. "There's a criminal organization he's been running; the clubs are a front, but we need to get the team in, they have to dig into it. If I do it, he'll trace it back to us. The asshole is slimy at best, but his contacts are fucking mafia and cartel."

"Jesus," I bite out, running my fingers through my short hair. "This needs to end. She doesn't need him in her life."

"And she needs you?" Finn challenges, his smirk curling his lips, and the flash of amusement in his eyes is evidence that my brother is attempting to taunt me.

"I never said she did. All I'm trying to do is help her, to make sure she's healthy, and alive. This bastard needs to pay for what he did to her." The anger in my tone is clear, thick and heavy with the threat of just what I'd love to do to the fucker when I get my hands on him. But as Finn said, we have to get as much information about him before making a move. I don't need the mafia or the fucking cartel coming to Thorne Haven.

"You want to be the hero she chooses in the end," Finn says nonchalantly. "You've always wanted to be that for her, and you can't deny it because I've known you your whole life. I've never seen you go off over a girl, or a woman, like this before."

"She's special," there's no need to deny it. If I did, I'd be lying.

"And you love her." This throws me for a moment, and my surprised gaze snaps to Finn's. "There's nothing wrong with love," he tells me with a smile; a chuckle vibrates in his chest. "But remember that when she heals, when she's healthy, she may want to move on from you. Don't put all your feelings into this because you could be the one getting hurt in the end."

"I don't need your advice, brother. You are the last person I should even consider taking advice from. When was the last time you had a girl in your life longer than one night?"

Finn shrugs. "I may not be the relationship type, but I know that happy endings don't always happen for everyone."

"It happened for Damien and Nesrin," I throw back easily. Our elder brother made a life for himself. He got his happy ending, something that everyone wants, but nobody realizes they need until it hits them right in the face.

"Yeah," Finn says, his gaze flicking to the floor before meeting mine once more. "But you're not Damien, and Kalyn is certainly not Nesrin." I know he's right, but we all have our own baggage, our own trauma.

"I need to go check on her," I say suddenly, earning me an arched brow from my brother. "Just to make sure she's not losing her mind. I don't know what he's got her on, and you saw her shaking like a leaf earlier."

"I did. It's not going to be easy," Finn tells me something I've already thought of, and that's why I need to be with her. I shouldn't have left her alone. "If you need anything..." He allows his words to trickle into silence, and all I can do is nod.

By the time I reach the door to the room Kalyn is in, I'm anxious about what I'm going to find. Attempting to be cold and aloof isn't going to work this time; I should've realized it earlier, but I'm out of my depth.

When I open the door and step inside, I find her curled on the bed, her body trembling, her whimpers alerting me to her state. My chest tightens when I look at her, so small, so fragile, and so strung out, she hasn't realized I've walked into the room yet.

I shut the door behind me and stalk toward her, hoping not to alarm her when I reach the bed. She's tossing and turning, and when she cries out, I reach for her, my fingertips trailing over her cheek. That's when her eyes snap open, and her gaze flicks up; a scream is wrenched from her throat that bounces against the four walls.

"Hey," I call to her, my hands out in an attempt to placate her. I woke her by accident, a nightmare clearly taking hold of her. "Look at me, Kaly," I speak, but her eyes are wide. How she transformed from a girl who could focus only an hour ago to someone who's so shattered is beyond me. "It's Cass," I tell her, praying with all I have that she recognizes me.

"Cass?" Her voice breaks, the pain that laces her words makes it difficult to breathe. Seeing her like this is not easy, I didn't expect it, but now that she's here, in front of me, I have to be strong for her.

"Yes, come here," I coo, keeping my voice low, a whisper, and the moment the words leave my lips, she's crawling over the mattress until she's cocooned in my arms. Her shaking doesn't subside immediately, and when I wrap my arms around her, I pull her into my body in the hopes that the warmth will ease her suffering somewhat.

Maybe he gave her something before she met with me because this makes no sense. She was shaking earlier, but now it's as if she has a fever, and my gut twists with nervous energy as I try to recall what was on the medical records Harris found.

Her whimpering calms the longer I hold her, and when

Kalyn stops shaking so violently, I lean back, trying to catch her focus. When those pretty eyes lock on me, she smiles a guilty, shy grin that makes my heart do stupid shit. She's the only girl who has ever made me feel any kind of emotion. Before her, and even with her, I never expected or wanted to have my heart twist in agony at her pain, or want to protect her like I now do.

"Would you like to take a hot shower?" I ask her, ensuring I don't raise my voice above a whisper. She hasn't moved from my arms, but the way her head tips up in my direction is evidence that she can hear me.

"Yes, please," Kaly whispers before nuzzling her face in the crook of my neck, and once again, that organ that's been hidden in a locked box for so many years thuds against my ribs, reminding me I can feel.

I lift her in my arms as if she were my bride and carry her to the attached bathroom. Setting her on the counter, I step away and take her in. There's a small grateful smile curling her lips, which makes me happy. She'll be okay; she's strong. All I need is for her to realize she has the strength to get through this.

I turn the taps on before turning back to her. "I'm going to be in the room. When you're done—"

"No, please!" Her voice is shrill with panic, her eyes widen as she looks up at me. "Just... Wait here." Her plea has my body and mind twisted with need because all I want is to see her strip down, but also, I know I can't touch her until she's healthy again. I don't want to fuck with her mind even more than that bastard Paulo's done.

"I'll... I mean, I don't—"

"Please, Cass," she pleads, her hands gripping my arms as she slides from the counter and drops to the floor in front of me. She's a head shorter than I am, so she has to tip her head back to look up at me.

"Okay," I finally appease her with a response, and she nods. Without another word, Kalyn strips down to her underwear, which is a barely-there scrap of panties that doesn't cover her ass but hides what I truly want to see. Her bra matches the color of her panties, and she slowly unhooks it, and I have to turn my gaze away, or I know I'll lose all control.

"Do you not like my body?" she asks, shocking me speechless, but I still don't turn to look at her because I'm almost certain she's naked. And if she is, I won't be able to restrain myself from touching her tonight.

"Of course, I do," I tell her honestly. "I just... I can't do this with you right now." The honest grit to my voice has her sighing before I hear the door sliding closed, and when I finally turn my head, I see she's behind the frosted glass. But even so, it doesn't hide the curves that tempt me from the other side.

Sighing quietly, I pull myself onto the counter and settle

in. I'm not sure how long she'll be in there, but I'll wait all night if I have to. I'm going to make sure that this woman is healed. Somehow, I'm going to ensure that what I failed to do when we were younger, I can accomplish now that I'm older and wiser.

The only thing that remains to be settled is her fiancé.

Tomorrow, shit is going to hit the fan, and when it does, I'm going to get blood on my hands. Paulo Morales's blood will coat my palms, and it will be satisfying to smell that metallic scent when I get vengeance for Kalyn.

Kalyn

THE WARM SPRAY OF THE SHOWER CALMS MY SHAKING, and for a long moment, I close my eyes and focus on just how good it feels to be warm. Cassian's arms holding me earlier was enough to have the shaking subside, but now with the hot shower beating down on my back, I'm feeling human again.

The need for something, a pill, a line of white powder still has its hold on me. I want nothing more than to fall into oblivion, but it won't happen while I'm here. I know Cassian and Finn are trying to help me, and I want to stop my addiction, but it's hard.

My body aches everywhere; even though I'm warmer

ice still trickles through me, reminding me that I'm a slave to the high. Tears burn my eyes when I think about it like that because I never wanted to be like this.

All I wanted was to forget my pain. But the older I got, the more agony took hold and the more I needed to inhale, to smoke, to drink just to clear my mind of the memories of all I've lost.

Shaking my head to clear my darkened thoughts, I focus on what's here and now. Glancing over my shoulder, I look at Cassian, whose head is turned away, his eyes on the counter instead of the shower. A small smile graces my expression as I grab the bottle of gel and fill my palm with some of the fragranced liquid. The gentle scent reminds me of Cassian—leather, cedar, and wood.

It's the smell of a warm, welcoming home. A place of safety. It calms me as I rub my body down and inhale deeply with my eyes closed as I focus on the warmth that's cocooning me, just like Cassian's arms did earlier on the bed.

When I open my eyes again, I find him watching me, which has my stomach tumbling with nervous energy. Never in my life did I think I'd be naked in the same room with Cassian Thorne. As friends, we've been in situations where we've been close, but he's never seen me in my underwear until moments ago. Never has he seen me like this, completely bared to him. And that's how I want him to see me, not like the girl he used to save from stupid decisions.

I want him to see me as a woman.

I should feel guilty for being engaged, but I don't.

Instead of that emotion eating away at me, excitement for what is slowly happening between Cass and me takes hold. I've loved him for most of my life, but we've never been ready for each other. Our time has never been right, but now, it has to be.

But I'm still wounded, deep inside. I need help, and for the first time in my life, I truly do want to heal. If I stand any chance with Cassian, I need to make sure I'm stronger than I've been in the past.

With Cassian's family paying for my dad's treatment, I can finally see the light at the end of the tunnel that I've been stuck in for so long. I have a chance to finally find peace, and I hope I can do it with Cassian by my side. If he still wants me.

I turn the taps off and open the door to find Cassian holding a towel out, his gaze averted. As I grab the fluffy material from his fingers, I want nothing more than for him to look at me. To see me all grown-up. But he doesn't give into temptation just yet.

"Thank you," I say as I wrap myself in the warmth of the towel. When he glances my way, it's cautious, and I know he's struggling with this new situation we find ourselves in.

From hating me, to wanting me to pay, to desire burning in his eyes, it's been a whirlwind of emotion these past few hours.

"I have some sweats and a shirt for you to wear. I'll get Joy to do a load of laundry in the morning. Your clothes will be dry before midday." He speaks as if he's unaffected by me, but the way those teal orbs drink me in, I know he's as turned on by this scene as I am.

"Thank you," I repeat my earlier sentiment because I can't find the words for how I'm feeling or what's going through my mind. I so want to sit with Cassian and talk, but fear has stolen my words. As much as I'd love for him to kiss me right now, to pull me into his arms, I know it's not the right time.

Although, it feels as if we've never had the right time to be what I believe we were meant to be. Since I was sixteen, I was under the impression that Cassian and I were destined. As a teen, I believed in fate; stupidly, I believed in happy ever afters. But then I realized they were only in fairy tales.

"Get dressed; I'll wait here," Cassian murmurs as he gestures to the bedroom where the clothes wait for me. I step by him, and I hear the inhale he takes. A deep breath of me as I pass him, which makes me smile.

By the time I reach the bed, I find a small tub of body lotion that I quickly rub on and pull the sweats up my legs. I'm shrugging on the tee when I feel his heat at my back.

"I want so much to take you right here, right now and claim you, to make you scream my name." His voice is a barely-there whisper. This time, it's the words he utters that make my body tremble, not the need for a high, but from the desire that's coursed through my veins for Cassian Thorne for most of my adult life. Well, since I was sixteen.

Age is only a number.

Isn't it?

"Then why don't you?" I taunt, wondering if he'll give into the tension that's swirling in the room, surrounding us like a fog. I want to get lost in the shadows with him, to finally experience just what he can do.

"Because when I do, there's no longer going to be any doubt who you belong to," Cassian admits, the seriousness of his tone taking over. His hands trail over my shoulders and down my arms. And then, his fingers are digging into my waist, gripping me harshly, and I welcome the pain that singes any thought of drugs, filling my mind with images of him.

"I never had any doubt about that, Cassian," I tell him easily because it's the truth. As stupid as that may seem, I always felt that he would be my first; when that didn't happen, I realized he never was meant to be my first. But now that I'm here, if I can heal myself, he can be my last.

"Then why did you lie?" he whispers in my ear, his lips trailing down the shell, causing goose bumps to erupt all over my body. "Why did you tell them I would force that shit on you?"

"I-I..." I'm not sure why. I can't even tell him the reason behind my stupidity that night because I, myself, don't know. "That night was a mistake, a big one. I was so angry at them making me leave, I lost control. After you dropped me at home, the pill I swallowed before the party hold of me and hit me hard. I was drunk, high, and yes, irresponsible. Even when I tried to make it right, to tell them it wasn't you, that I lied, they didn't listen. My father found out—"

"And he was disappointed in his little princess?" Cassian taunts, and I shut my eyes tightly to keep the tears of shame at bay. He's right. There's no doubt I've always wanted my father's approval. I spent years wanting to see the look of pride on his face when he regarded me.

"Yes." My admission is filled with bitter guilt.

Cassian spins me around, causing me to gasp in surprise. When I glance up at him, I find anger swirling with desire in his eyes. The look of a man who's about to devour his prey is painted on his handsome face. I want to close my eyes and not see the attack. But instead of cowering, I look him dead in the eye and wait.

"Get on your knees," Cassian orders in a voice dripping with lust and desire. There's no debating what's about to happen, so I obey, lowering myself to my knees. I look up to see the bulge that's so clearly prominent in his tight, black jeans.

I can't help but squirm at the sight, and a chuckle from Cassian tells me he's seen my weakness. He knows how much I want him, how many years I've craved this. His hand tangles in my wet curls, and he tugs my head back as he leans forward, so we're eye to eye.

"Don't think this is because I want you," he grits through clenched teeth. "You're here because I abhor men like Paulo, but I never claimed to be better."

"You said you wanted to be the hero," I force out the words he spoke earlier. "My hero." At my admission, he releases me quickly, stepping away as he runs his other hand through the barely-there crop of dark hair.

"I shouldn't have done that," he says, but he doesn't look at me. "You're fragile. You're—"

"I'm not broken, Cassian," I grind out confidently through clenched teeth as I push to my feet. "I may have a weakness for a high, but I'm not broken." I want to taunt this man, to push him to his limit and see him lose control. For years he kept himself restrained around me. But I'm tired of him treating me like I'm made of glass.

"Then why do I feel like I'm about to shatter your world?" he asks as he turns to face me. His expression is pained, his eyes still dancing with desire, and his lips, they're curled at the corners.

"Because you have the power to do that," I admit. It's not

like he didn't know how I felt about him. I told him enough times over the years. Granted, we haven't seen each other for a while, but he knew. He still knows. I never hid anything from him. Of everyone in my life, Cassian is the only person who knows every sordid detail about me.

He turns to face me fully. This time, there's a seriousness etched on his handsome face that makes me nervous. But then he asks, "Then why do you allow me that power?"

Cassian

I DON'T KNOW WHY I ASK HER THAT, BUT I HAVE TO KNOW. She's always given me the power to possibly break her heart, and perhaps, without knowing, I did. She never once said anything about it, she never told me I hurt her, but deep down, I can't help but wonder if I inadvertently did when I told her we couldn't be anything more because she wasn't eighteen.

I was always cautious about our friendship. Even though there was flirting, obvious desire, we never acted on it. Her eyes are wide as she focuses on me. Her earlier need for drugs seems to have mellowed out, for now. But tonight, when she's in bed alone, she'll crave it. I know. I've seen it happen with others.

"I didn't think you would be the one to break my heart," she finally responds, and I realize her words are guarded. There's an admission so clear in her answer, and my own chest tightens at the thought of me hurting her.

"We never spoke about feelings, emotions," I tell her honestly. Over the years, she never hid how she felt; that much was clear, but she never once openly voiced her feelings for me. She hit on me when she was drunk or high, but I always put it down to the shit she put in her bloodstream.

"We didn't." She nods slowly. "But there was never an indication that I didn't want you. I've always been yours, Cassian. You owned me before I even knew what that meant."

Shaking my head, I offer a small smile. "You were too young to even know what those kinds of emotions were." I reach for her face, my hand cupping her cheek, and she nuzzles into my touch as if I were her anchor to this world, rooting her to the here and now.

"Perhaps. But I also knew that my heart was stronger when I was with you; I felt at ease in my own shoes when I walked beside you, more than any other time in my life. And I breathed easier when you were around. The only person who understood me was you."

This time, when Kaly looks at me, there are no lies, there's no fog of a high in her pretty eyes. She's not lying, and it does things to me. Things I don't want to admit or allow myself to feel. But I don't have a choice because all I can see or smell, or feel, is her.

"I may have been young, sort of innocent, but I knew what I felt in my heart, Cassian," she admits softly, her lips capturing my thumb, and I watch with pure lust coursing through my veins as she sucks the digit into her warm mouth. Her teeth scraping along the flesh, sending desire straight to my hardening erection.

"Kaly." Her name is a warning. "Little liar," I say, calling her the nickname I've given her since *that* night. "Don't tease me."

This time, I see the girl I once knew when she locks her gaze with mine. "Why? Because you'll finally give in to what you've always wanted?" she teases and bites down on my thumb hard until my cock throbs against my zipper.

My mind is awash with all the ways I can make her cry and scream. Pushing her back until she hits the mattress, I'm on her in a second. My body looming over her smaller one.

Thankfully she'd already gotten dressed because if she'd been in the towel, it would've fallen open, and I would've been knocked breathless by the sight of her naked beneath me.

"This isn't the way it should happen," I tell her earnestly.

Kaly shakes her head. "Why? Because it's against the rules?" This time, it's another one of her sassy remarks, those that always got her into trouble around me.

I watched for years as she came into her own with the boys at school. Though none of them were confident enough to take it too far because I had my Haven boys, along with my two brothers, watching her like hawks.

But there was always one or two guys hanging around, hoping to get lucky. They never did. I made sure of it. Kaly doesn't know what I did in school to keep her virtue safe. Deep down, I wanted it for myself, but now that I know that ship has sailed, I know I can't be her first, but I'll most definitely be her last.

"I never wanted you to hurt, to feel pain, but when your grandmother died, and you went over the edge, all I could do was be there for you," I tell her. I recall those dark days easily because they will always be stuck in my mind, reminding me of just how difficult loss is.

"You could've healed me."

"By what? Fucking you?" I bite out as frustration takes hold. I spent nights alone thinking of her then. I would drop her at home after the parties she loved to frequent, and when I did, I always wanted to follow her inside. I wanted to see her flop onto her bed and fall asleep. I didn't need those cheerleaders who so clearly wanted me; all I craved was Kalyn. "I'm sorry."

"No, you're right. There wasn't anything else you could offer me," she grits as the anger drips from her words. Shoving away from her, I put distance between us. The cold of her not being snug against me hits me hard. And I miss it. I miss her softness.

I glance at her from over my shoulder. "I shouldn't have said that. I didn't mean it like that," I murmur. "I just didn't see a way out of the darkness."

For a long moment, she's silent. I watch as she slides onto the bed, tugging the comforter over her body. Her eyes are still on me, watching me as if I'm about to disappear. But I don't. I settle in the wingback chair and keep my attention on her.

"There was a lot of darkness back then," Kalyn says. "But there's so much more now. If you would've just admitted what you felt back then." It's not an accusation, but it still bites right down to my gut. Perhaps if I had told her how I felt, things wouldn't be so fucked-up.

"Maybe," I acquiesce. "Go to sleep."

She lifts her head for a moment before asking, "Will you stay?" She doesn't reach for me, and I don't go to her, but I realize she doesn't want to be alone. I ponder her request. Her expression pleading silently, and I nod.

"Yes, I'll be here all night." I shouldn't stay because if I do, the temptation to finally taste her will be too much. But I can't leave her alone. Not when she's struggling.

She's trembling as she slips under the covers, and I realize it's going to be a tough night.

"How long has he been feeding you that shit?" I ask, praying she says it's nothing too serious.

But then she responds, "All the time I've known him. Pretty much every night to get me to sleep." Her voice is soft, broken, and my chest tightens both with the need to protect her and the ache to kill Paulo with my bare hands. I want to rip him to shreds.

Her head hits the pillow gently before her lashes flutter along the apples of her cheeks. Silence descends, and I'm able to finally take her in.

Her beauty has always astounded me. She's a natural. She doesn't need makeup, or injections, or any of that other shit girls in this town think are what men want. Kalyn is pure, in every fucking way.

My jeans tighten as her soft breaths escape her plump lips, and I have to shut my eyes to focus on something other than how good her warmth would feel right now.

Her phone buzzes on the nightstand, and I quickly push to my feet to grab it. Swiping the screen, I open the message and grin.

When you get home, we need to have a talk. I'm not happy.

Don't worry, motherfucker, I'm coming for you, and I'm not happy either.

Kalyn

WHEN I WAKE UP, I'M ALONE. FOR A MOMENT, I'M confused about where I am, but the moment I look around, I realize I'm still at the Thorne mansion. Last night was exhausting. My need for a high hit me, but Cassian walked in and offered me solace in the form of confessions. He finally openly admitted it; the truth was in his words, in his affection. He wanted me as much as I did him, and even now, he still wants me.

There's no longer a doubt in my mind that he is the one. Only, I have so much baggage to deal with before I can even think about being with Cassian. The tension in the room from last night still lingers, and I wonder just how long it's going to be before I can go home.

He wants me to stay here, but I have to face Paulo. I can't disappear and expect him to just accept it. There'll be anger, threats, and violence, I have no doubt. But I wonder if Cassian's going to do something. Last night, he vowed to kill the man.

Ice takes hold of my veins, and I close my eyes once more, focusing on my breathing before a panic attack takes over. I don't want Cassian to get into trouble because of me, again.

He may have helped me last night, but it's time I fought my own battles. I'd love to lie in bed all day and ignore what's happening around me. But I can't. I have to be an adult and face this. No matter how difficult.

I push to my feet as the door slides open and Cassian steps into the room. He's dressed in a black suit with a white button-up that's undone, offering a view of smooth, tanned skin.

His eyes are sparkling with something I can't quite put my finger on. He sets down a tray he's holding that has breakfast on it, including a mug of steaming coffee and a bottle of chilled water.

"I thought you might be hungry," he says with a smile that steals my breath and has my heart thudding wildly against my ribs.

"Thank you," I say, padding barefoot to where he's set down the tray. I grab the water and quickly swallow down a few mouthfuls before looking at Cassian who's watching me with amusement. "What?"

"I just like looking at you," he says.

Narrowing my gaze, I ask, "What happened to making me pay for my lie?" I pick up the mug of coffee and bring it to my lips as I wait for his answer.

Cassian shrugs it off before walking to the chair he sat in last night. He settles in comfortably before saying, "I will ensure you've paid for that, but for now, we're going to sort out the other shit going on in your life."

"Has Paulo called? Has he figured out I'm here?" I sit on the bed, facing Cassian as he shakes his head. "Then what's happened? Is my father doing okay?"

"Yes, he's fine. I've got my men watching him. Don't worry so much. The first thing we do need to sort out is Paulo. Once he's out of the picture, you'll be mine. Without any other complications."

My mouth falls open; shock must be clear on my expression, judging by Cassian's chuckle. He rests his left ankle on his right knee before pulling out his cell phone and taps out something. When he's done, he lands his focused gaze on me.

"So, tell me more about this man you agreed to marry," he says. "I've done some research, and it seems he's settling into the Narro home as if it's his."

I was afraid Paulo wouldn't want to sell. My folks need

the money. And the only way for them to get free of his hold is if they can pay back the money Dad owes Paulo. The problem is, when he saw the house upon our arrival, he said something that clicked in my mind—*It could be a good base for us.*

"He wants to ensure we're forever indebted to him. I'm not sure why. My father owes him a lot of money. They've known each other for a while, but I don't know why Paulo is holding my family hostage."

"You think perhaps your father had a gambling problem? Or something more... sinister?" Cassian asks, and my throat closes with anxiety. I didn't want to admit it, but the moment Dad introduced me to Paulo, something felt off. I didn't allow myself to think about it too long. But now that Cassian's said it, I can't deny it any longer.

"I'm not sure, but I wouldn't put it past him. Dad's always been a prideful man, and when he lost all that money, he said he'd do anything to get it back. And that's what makes me wonder if Paulo didn't step in before he met me."

Cassian nods slowly, his expression filled with thought as he pulls out his phone once more and taps on the screen. "I'll have the men look into it. I didn't consider that possibility until you mentioned it."

"What are you going to do about Paulo?" I ask before sipping the hot liquid, enjoying the warmth as it fills my belly. But even though I'm enjoying the coffee, nervous energy flutters along with the warmth.

"I'm going to make him pay," Cassian says nonchalantly as if he's talking about the weather. "He's coming here for a meeting under the impression we have a deal for him. Once he's in my house, on my property, I'll ensure he doesn't leave until I've questioned him and got a confession about what he did to you."

"What if he doesn't confess?" I don't doubt Cassian's good at what he does, and the men he has working for him will probably get the job done, but deep down, uncertainty sits like a lead weight on my chest.

The corner of his mouth tips upward, and ice trickles from my neck down to the base of my spine, causing me to shiver. I've never seen this side of Cassian before. All the years we'd been friends, he was always level-headed, calm and relaxed. But right now, I'm seeing the other side of him, and it's feral.

"I'll ensure the bastard talks," he assures me. "I have my ways. It's best if you don't know what we're doing."

"Are you...? Are you going to hurt him? Like, would you kill him?"

Cassian glances at me, his stare dancing with answers I probably don't want to know as he regards me, and I can tell there would be no lie in what his response would be.

"I'll do whatever I must to ensure you're safe again," he confesses before he pushes to his feet. I want to grab him, to keep him here with me. But I don't. I watch him move through the room before he stops at the windows. "Are you feeling okay?" he asks, but doesn't look at me.

"Last night was difficult, I had some strange dreams, nightmares, but this morning I do feel better. I *think* I can do this." My admission has Cassian turning to face me, his expression filled with pride, and my chest aches for him to come to me, to finally claim me like I know he wants to.

"Good," he says. "I know you can. Since I first met you, I knew you were strong, Kaly." A small smile dances on his face before he looks away, robbing me of his handsome face. "I need to go," he announces suddenly and turns from the window.

"Wait," I call out as he reaches the door. I pad quietly over to him, stopping inches from his body, feeling his warmth without meaning to. Cassian's always been warm to me, soothing as if he were a security blanket, and without him, these past few years have been hell.

Cass glances over his shoulder, his hand on the doorknob as he watches me. His brow arches in question, waiting for me to speak, and suddenly, I'm nervous. I haven't felt the butterflies in my stomach for so long; it's strange.

"Come back to me," I finally tell him, hoping I don't sound like a stupid little girl who's still holding onto a teenage crush.

The corner of his mouth tilts into one of those familiar

smiles. The same one that used to turn me into a bumbling idiot when I was lucky enough to be gifted with it. Cassian is older now, all grown-up, and yet, he still makes me feel like that sixteen-year-old girl falling for her best friend.

"I'll always come back for you," he affirms before disappearing, leaving me with thoughts and memories that hold me hostage. Cassian Thorne may have the self-control of a priest, but that night, he admitted to wanting me. It was the only time he ever let go of his restraint.

The sun is high in the sky, and lunch is almost ready. Thankfully being invited to the Thorne manor isn't as scary as it used to be. The first time I walked into the enormous mansion, I felt so small, as if I was invading a sacred space. But now, I'm here, and it's as if I belong.

Damien saunters from the kitchen, his blue gaze catching mine. "Little Kaly," he says with a smile that sends my stomach tumbling wildly. All three Thorne brothers are beautiful, breathtaking, and even though the eldest one looks like an Adonis, it's the middle brother, my best friend, who has my mind running wildly.

I offer a shy smile. "Hello, Damien," I greet him. Most girls at school can't get a word out when he's around. And I can see why. He's dressed all in black, reminding me of a vampire about to feast on my blood.

"He's out back," he informs me, knowing I'm here for Cassian.

"Thanks," I mumble as I rush by him, my cheeks hot from

embarrassment. When I reach the back porch, I take in the number of students already at the pool. At first, I didn't want to come here, to be surrounded by people I didn't fit in with, but Cassian promised to look after me.

As he always does.

"There she is," he says when he sees me, leaving the grill to Finn. When he reaches me, his arm snakes around my neck, and he pulls me into his hold. Since I turned seventeen a couple of weeks ago, he's been holding me more often. Being affectionate, whereas when we first met, he never came close to me.

"Quite the party," I remark, watching the girls in tiny bikinis as they splash around in the pool, and I'm jealous, wanting to be that comfortable in my own skin.

"It is. But you're here now, so it's even better," Cassian whispers in my ear, sending heat coursing through my body. If he only knew how I truly felt. "Want something to drink?"

"You have the hard stuff?" I tease, looking up into those endless teal eyes.

He chuckles, and I bask in the vibration from his chest. "You can have one drink, but only one." His warning is clear. Cass knows I drink and get high. He's been there on more than one occasion when I've been out of my mind. He's been my rock, holding me steady.

When he hands me some fruity drink, I can't help but roll my eyes, earning myself another chuckle. I sip the fizzy drink and linger around, keeping close to Cassian because the rest of the kids are all a year older than me, which has me nervous to talk to any of them.

The darker the sky gets, the rowdier the party, and as soon as the sky has burst with a prickling of white stars, there are couples skinny dipping in the pool, some have taken to the hot tub. I lean back in one of the loungers when a couple of guys surround me, one has a joint, which he offers me, and I thankfully accept.

After a few pulls on it, I feel the high hitting my veins, taking me to a place where my anxiety no longer exists, and soon, I'm shimmying out of my jean shorts and tank top. Underneath is a bright green bikini that barely covers what needs to be hidden.

I'm about to head for the pool when a firm grip on my hips startles me, causing a yelp to tumble from my lips. The warm breath of someone is at my ear in seconds, and then his voice cuts through my high.

"What the fuck are you wearing?" Cassian hisses with a threat of danger in his voice. His lips send electricity zipping down my body like sparks from a firework setting off to burn me alive.

"A bikini," I sass him, tugging away so I can face him. When I do manage to spin around, my breath is knocked from my lungs when I take in his thundering expression. "What?"

"You're not fucking wearing that," he grits as his hand snags my arm and picks up my clothes with the other before he pulls me into the house, all the way up the stairs until we're in his bedroom. Alone. The word trickles through my mind, and my thighs squeeze together at the possessiveness in his eyes.

"What's wrong with this? The other girls have similar—"

"You're not the other fucking girls," he says, pushing me up against his bedroom door. I've only ever been in here once before. And right now, I'm practically naked while he's still fully clothed. I'm at quite the disadvantage.

Tipping my head back, I lift my chin before I ask, "What does that mean?"

His hands land on the door behind me, his arms caging me in. I want so much for him to kiss me. I can't stop myself from lifting onto my tiptoes, so I'm taller. Even so, I'm still shorter than him.

"Why are you acting like this?" I whisper, my words feathering from my lips to his. The tension in the room is heavy, my head spins from the weed, and while I try to appear confident, I know for a fact he can see past my act. He affects me. It's never been a secret.

"You're fucking mine," he confesses. "I don't want other men looking at what's mine." His words wash over me for a moment, warming every inch of me, causing my thighs to once more squeeze together.

Cassian doesn't miss the movement as his eyes drop to my legs. "Does that make your pussy wet?" he taunts, lowering his voice to a gravely hiss. "Do you like that I'm so fucking obsessed with you?"

"I-I..." No words come out because I've never heard him admit how he feels. Our friendship has been easy; we fell into sync as if we were made to know each other. Over the time I've known Cassian, I've shamelessly flirted with him, but he's always kept me at arm's length.

He's so close. His mouth is inches from mine. If I were to move forward, barely an inch, I would finally have what I've always wanted—a kiss. But I don't. Because this isn't how it's meant to happen. Call me a girl with my head in the clouds, but I want Cassian to kiss me. Not the other way around.

The air in the room is filled with sexual tension, and my stomach twists as he leans in but misses my lips by a hairsbreadth; instead, he runs his warmth over my cheek. "I thought so," he finally says before pushing away from me. "Put your clothes on; I'll be back." He heads to a door to our left, which I'm guessing is an en-suite bathroom.

"Will you?" I challenge from the door with my hands trembling and my knees weak as I try to keep from collapsing.

Before he shuts himself inside, he glances over his shoulder, a smirk playing on his lips. "I'll always come back for you."

Cassian

B Y THE TIME I GET TO THE LIVING ROOM, I'M STILL HARD, still wanting to claim the girl in the bedroom down the hall. When I step into the room, Finn glances up from talking to Harris. Both men watch me as I settle in the chair overlooking the table where the laptops are set up.

"She's worried he won't confess," I say, my voice still scratchy from my talk with Kalyn. "I want this bastard taken down as soon as possible. Do we have the evidence?" This time, I lift my attention toward Harris, who nods.

"I have video evidence from one of the partygoers. It clearly shows Morales injecting Kalyn with something. Obviously, we're not able to know what was in the syringe, but later that night, more videos were taken by attendees showing her not in the best condition."

This piques my interest, but it also skyrockets my rage. "What do you mean?"

He sets down an iPad on the table in front of me and taps play on the video. On screen, Kalyn is dancing with a few girls at a party. Her head lolling side to side, and she doesn't seem to be with it. My blood simmers at the sight. I've seen her like that before, but at the time, she was a kid, and I pulled her into my car and took her home.

Every time she lost her fight, I was there, fighting for her.

"I want Morales locked up," I tell Harris. "I want him downstairs, chained to the wall so we can question him."

"The team is here for you, Cassian," he tells me. The older man, who I've known all my life, has seen me grow into the person I am today. He's seen my heartbreaks, my anger, and he's seen my rage. When my father wasn't around, Harris was. I glance up at him, and I don't have to tell him what I want done, because he already knows.

The crunching of gravel outside is our evidence that Paulo is here. It doesn't take long for Harris's men to make a beeline for the BMW that's pulled up at our door. I listen to the footsteps, then the door whooshes open with curse words flying from Paulo's mouth.

"What the fuck is this? What fucking bullshit are you planning here?" He struggles to get free, and I note that

Harris has four men surrounding him. He's not going anywhere. I push to my feet before making my way to our guest.

"Mr. Morales," I greet as I button up my suit jacket. With an image of Kalyn in a state of drunkenness in my mind, I rear my hand back and make contact with the asshole's face, earning me a sickening crunch of bone under my knuckles.

Blood drips from his nose when Paulo turns his attention back to me. "You bastard, I'll fucking kill you," he threatens, causing me to chuckle.

"You can try," I inform him. "But I think you'll listen to me because I have enough evidence to take you and your organization down. And if you'd like to perhaps see the light of day again, you'll accompany my men so we can have a little... chat," I tack on the last word with a grin that is void of humor. Instead, I pin him with a hate-filled glare.

"Fuck you." His eyes burn with rage. It doesn't faze me because I'm sure by the time this day is over, he'll be a whimpering bitch on his knees before me. The men lead him down toward the basement, and I watch while standing beside Finn.

"Did you enjoy that?" my brother asks, amusement clear in his tone. I know he's talking about the punch I got in before we even had a chance to get the asshole downstairs.

"I did." Taking in the mess on the floor, I know Joy is going to be angry because she'll have to clean it up. But I needed to let out just an ounce of aggression, or I wouldn't be able to get through the interrogation.

I make my way down to the basement, with Finn and Harris hot on my heels. With every step, I get even more anxious because as much as I enjoy doing this shit, it's not easy.

In the cold basement, I take in Paulo, who's now bound against the brick wall, which has four metal cuffs that lock both wrists and both ankles in place. He's mine, and I'm going to make him scream like a little bitch for what he did to my girl.

"Now," I start as I head for the cabinet against the one wall that houses a few implements we brought down here years ago. "I'd like to talk about your fiancée. I'm sure you remember her."

"Is that bitch talking about me?" Paulo sneers, and I'm tempted to end him right here and now, but I glance at Finn who's shaking his head slowly in warning. We do need more of a confession than his hatred for the woman he's engaged to.

"Eight months ago, you did something that I'd like to talk about." I grab what I need and turn to Paulo.

His eyes are on mine. I can see the confusion dancing in his dark eyes. "I don't know what you're talking about."

I take a few steps, bringing me closer to him, but the distance is enough so that if I want to use the pliers in my hand, I can. "You know what I'm talking about because Kalyn is still healing from your lack of interest in her health and being more concerned with keeping her high."

"She's nothing more than an addict. She likes it, begs me for it. Is that what you want to hear? When she drops to her knees and pleads for me to fuck her face like the whore she is." His words send pure fury racing through my veins, and I nod my head to one of the men who grabs Paulo's jaw. He opens it wide enough for me to get a good grip on two of the bastard's teeth, and I pull swiftly. Blood spurts from the wounds and pours from his mouth, and pained cries bounce off the walls.

"I think you need to truly consider your next answer," I warn him as the echoes of his blubbering make me smile. Causing pain to bastards like him can be satisfying. However, this is a special case because I have an interest in the woman he's hurt. I don't doubt Kalyn wasn't the first, and if I allow him to continue, she won't be the last.

"She'll never survive without me," he splutters, the words gurgled as his mouth fills with crimson liquid. He lifts his gaze, locking his dark eyes on mine. "She needs me."

"That's where you're wrong." Keeping my cool comes easy; I take a step back to take in my handiwork. Crossing my arms in front of my chest, I smile as I tip my head to the side. "Now. Are you ready to talk?"

"There's nothing to say," he tells me. "She's my fiancée,

and I've taken care of her family since we met."

"That's what I don't understand. You chose a random girl, told her you'll pay for her father's medical treatment, and marry her. That sounds like a saint if I ever heard of one. It doesn't make sense." I've tried to figure it out since I heard Kalyn's story. Yes, her addiction has been a pull for Paulo. But what doesn't make sense is why someone like him would offer to help her father. Unless her father is indebted to Paulo in some way.

"If you can't figure it out, pretty boy, then you're as stupid as you look," Paulo mumbles before spitting a mouthful of blood on the floor right at my feet. He's trying to anger me once more, but for now, I keep my cool.

"I've been very nice to you," I inform him before stepping closer. Another nudge of my chin, and his mouth is pried open once more. "But I'm getting tired of waiting for you to admit just what you did to Kalyn."

I don't want to mention the pregnancy. If I do, the admission could be inadmissible because I've goaded him into it. I want him to admit it on his own accord.

I clamp the tip of his tongue between the metal teeth. "I think you need to think long and hard about what your next answer is going to be because I wouldn't think twice about cutting you to pieces. And even then, I think that's far too good for you."

I open the grip of the pliers and step back, allowing my

guy to release Paulo's jaw. "That bitch was trying to trap me in some happy family," he finally admits half of what I need. "I wasn't having it."

Shaking my head at his words, I ask, "And what exactly did you think you'd do once you walked down the aisle? You were engaged to her anyway."

He grins. A sinister smile as his gums that are still bleeding cause him to look manic. His eyes are wild with animalistic rage. "She thinks I was going to walk down that aisle and make her happy." He chuckles, spitting more blood in order to continue speaking. "The day of our wedding, my men would've ensured she learned the truth."

Rage explodes in my gut, and I swing the tool in my hand, making contact with his knee, which cracks under the metal of the pliers. Another scream of pure agony surrounds us as Paulo's leg sways. I should've used the hammer, but that would mean walking away from him. And right now, it's taking all my restraint not to murder him in cold blood. "What?"

"I fucking killed that fetus she was so happily carrying so she could die with nothing but regret in her pretty white dress. Did you know blood looks so much better on white?" he sneers, and that's when I lose all self-control. All I see is red. My vision is blurred. I lift my hand with the pliers, swinging it at his face, the crunch of bone, the scream of pain that fills my ears doesn't stop me.

I can't stop.

I don't know how many times I hit him, but soon, heavy hands are dragging me away from the unconscious man hanging by his wrists that are bound in metal cuffs.

"Cass," Finn's voice breaks through the dark cloud in my mind. "Cass, look at me." He cups my face, and when I meet his worried gaze, I finally breathe deeply. The scent of iron is all I can smell. My hands are shaking, my body is trembling.

"I-I'm f-fine."

Finn shakes his head, before helping me to my feet and dragging me up the stairs until we reach the foyer where we walk straight into my dad. His brows arch as he takes us in. I glance down and realize I'm drenched in blood. Paulo's blood.

I don't know if he's alive. But I don't care.

"Do I need to know what this is about?" Dad questions as he steps toward me, reaching for my face.

"No." It's all I can manage as I look into my father's eyes. He's been around violent men before. My dad knows some of the worst assassins in the world, and Thorne Industries hires them from time to time, so blood and violence aren't new to Dad.

But it's only one of a few times he's seen me coming from the basement. I've questioned men down there before, but none have bled like this. None of them have fallen victim to my rage like Paulo Morales.

"If you need help," Dad says finally.

"We're okay; I need to get him cleaned up," Finn says because I can't find my words. Dad nods, allowing us to make our way up to my bedroom, but I want to see her. I want to go to Kalyn and tell her I've got all I need to ensure her safety.

I want to tell her I'm the hero in her story.

"Go shower. You can't go see her like this."

"Why?" I challenge, turning to face Finn, who's looking at me like he's seen a ghost. "Because I'm wearing the blood of her fiancé?" My voice is dark, husky with frustration. Pushing by Finn, I ignore his pleas as I make my way down the hall, taking the stairs two at a time.

Rushing down the long hallway that will take me to Kalyn, I stop outside her bedroom door and glance over at my brother, who followed me and is watching me with wariness in his gaze.

"I'm done waiting."

Three words I've wanted to say in years. I expect Finn to tell me to stop, to not go inside, but with my admission, he realizes how much I need this, and he nods.

"I get it," he finally whispers. "Just... be careful," he warns, and I know he's referring to the moment I claim her. I've waited so long, I'm not sure how much restraint I can hold onto because, right now, I'm feral. All I want is to feel her, in my hands, underneath me, and I'm starving to get a taste of the girl who's haunted my fucking dreams for eight long years.

I unlock and push open the door. Leaving Finn in the hallway, I shut myself inside the bedroom. Kalyn looks up from where she's sitting on the windowsill. Her attention was on the window, but now, it's on me, and my blood heats for another reason than it was earlier.

Right now, it's burning with desire.

"It's done."

She's on her feet at my confession. She rushes toward me, her eyes widening when she takes in my appearance. The blood that's dried on my hands, my face, and clothes are a clear indication of what I did for her. I needed her to see this side of me.

For years, I hid my desire for violence from her. From everyone except my brothers. But now, she's seeing who I am. The part of me I've always kept at bay when I've been around her.

"What happened?" she whispers, her hand reaching for me, and when her fingertips make contact with my cheek, I can't hold back anymore.

I grip her wrist, earning me a dick-hardening gasp. Spinning us around, so Kalyn is pressed against the door, I pin her with my hips, and another whimper falls free from her plump lips when she feels my hardness against her thigh.

"I've saved you once again, little liar," I murmur along her lips, but I don't kiss her. Not yet. "It's time for your payment."

"What payment?" Kalyn whimpers when I push my thigh between her legs. Her heat is the remedy to my bruises, and I know her taste will be the sweetest fucking drug I'll ever take.

"You know what you need to atone for," I whisper before I tangle my fingers in her soft hair and tug her closer. Her plump lips part on a moan, and I finally steal what I've been craving for far too long. The suppleness of her body molds to me, my hardness against her soft feminine curves, and it's as if I'm being tugged toward solace.

Tonight, I'm getting high, I'm finally going to take everything this woman has to offer, and I'm not giving anything back.

Kalyn

MY BODY IS HIS. EVERY INCH OF ME HAS MOLDED TO Cassian's sculpted torso as he finally kisses me, and as his tongue dances with mine, my mind goes blank, and my lungs struggle to work.

His hands trail down to my hips, and he grips me so hard, I'm certain there'll be bruises tomorrow. He moves his hands to my ass, lifting me against him, pinning me against the wooden surface of the door, as he steals every moan and whimper that he elicits from my body.

My fingers trail over his soft, short, cropped hair in an attempt to pull him closer, to bring him nearer, but there's no way to do so because we're connected in such a way; it's as if we're one.

When Cassian finally breaks the kiss, my lips feel swollen from his assault, my body is trembling with the need for more. I don't know why he's stopped, why he's pulling away, but I try to tug him closer, but he slowly shakes his head.

My panties are soaked. Instinctively, my hips roll in an attempt to find friction, causing Cassian to chuckle. "My little liar wants to come?" he taunts, his dark brow arching as he regards me with amusement.

"Is this my punishment?" I whisper, my voice croaky with every word I utter, and my cheeks burn because he's affected me so much, I'd do anything for him to finish what he just started.

"This is not at all your punishment; this is my reward," he tells me earnestly. "You see all this blood?" I nod in response to his question. "This is what I did for you. That bastard will not be hurting you again."

"What happened?"

Cassian shakes his head. "You don't need to know. All that matters is he's out of your life, which means you're now single," he informs me, and I realize that's why he's finally come in here and kissed me. All this time, he's been teasing, waiting, and biding his time until he wasn't doing anything that would bring about guilt in either of us.

I'm not cheating.

I'm free.

"What about my dad's treatments?" I ask again. Even though I recall Cassian saying the Thornes will be footing the bill, I need to know; I need another confirmation.

"Like I said, you're mine now, little liar," Cassian says, his tone warm yet calculated and serious. "And everything in your life belongs to me, whether it's a bill that needs to be paid or a man that needs to be killed."

"You killed him?" I gasp in shock. There's a lot of blood on his clothes, but I didn't think Cassian would actually do it.

"Not yet," he appeases me. "He's in just a little.... *pain*," he whispers the last word, which is drenched in a threat I don't want information about.

"So... You're... I mean, we're..." I don't know how to word it, how to ask him if it means he wants me. I want to ask him if I'm his now, does that mean he's mine too?

Cassian tips his head to the side, his eyes narrow to quizzical teal orbs as he watches me, drinking in every inch of my face. "What is it, little liar?"

"Are we a couple?" I ask, feeling stupid for even voicing it because I sound like a child. A teen with a crush on the popular boy in school. And his hands are still gripping my ass as if he's going to mark me for life.

"I'll have to think about it." He chuckles when my mouth falls open at his response. "Let's just say we'll take it a day at a time because right now, I'm going to strip all these clothes off your body, and I'm going to taste every inch of you. And when you're a whimpering mess, begging for my cock inside you, I might give you what you've wanted since you were sixteen."

"You're such a bastard," I bite out, swatting him on the shoulder, only earning me a smile in response. He knows what I want, what I need, so when Cassian spins on his heel with me still in his hold, I'm not scared. Not anymore.

Cassian drops me onto the mattress with a bounce, and a squeal escapes me. He leans in, and I instinctively scoot back, but he's on me in seconds. His body nestles between my thighs, and his hardness presses against my core, sending pleasure shooting through every inch of me.

"Time to see just how sweet my little liar tastes," he murmurs as he tugs at the sweatpants that he gave me to wear. His fingers hook into my panties, and he grins when I gasp, feeling the cool air hitting my body. Cassian's movements are swift, and seconds later, my waist, all the way down to my toes, is bared before him.

His pupils dilate when he drinks me in. His hands grip my ankles, and he lifts both to his mouth, sending me sprawling on the mattress. His lips press soft kisses on each leg before he lowers my feet to the bed.

I watch as he shrugs off his jacket; next to disappear is his button-up shirt, which is stained with blood. And then I'm met with Cassian's body. Broad shoulders that have lean muscles tensing as he moves. His chest is smooth, tanned, and every inch of him is sculpted to perfection.

My gaze drinks him in, trailing down to his abs that look like they've been chiseled from marble. His hips taper down into his pants, and the V muscles make my mouth water. There's a dark trail of hair under his belly button that leads down, behind the waistband of his suit pants.

"Enjoying the view?" he taunts confidently, clearly enjoying the attention.

"Not bad." My sass earns me a light swat on my thigh. "Hey!"

"Off with the top," he orders easily, and for once in my life, I don't retort a response or challenge him; I simply obey. The moment the material hits the bed beside me, Cassian is on me, over me, consuming my every thought and breath.

His hands on the mattress on either side of my head cage me in. His mouth inches from mine, the warmth of him cocooning me, and then he rolls his hips, sending sparks of pure pleasure shooting from my core to every nerve ending in my body.

"Cassian." His name slips unbidden from my lips when his mouth captures the sensitive flesh of my neck, and he suckles hard until I'm a whimpering mess. I know he's marking me, and I haven't been more turned on than I am right now.

He doesn't answer. His response is his movement down my body, capturing a hardened nipple between his teeth as he bites down, turning me inside out as he sends more pleasure skittering down my spine, causing my clit to throb for contact. Still, he doesn't offer satisfaction; he merely taunts.

Each kiss is nothing but a tease. When he reaches my stomach, I feel the chuckle in response to my hips lifting involuntarily at his nearness to where I need him most.

"Is my little liar aching?" he questions, and when I open my eyes, I find those teal orbs looking up at me from between my thighs, and everything I want to throw back at him in response disappears.

Memories of nights where I was alone in bed, my fingers pleasuring me as my fantasies of Cassian teased me, hitting me full force. All I can do is nod, and he smiles a grin that makes him look like a feral animal ready to feast.

And feast he does.

His mouth latches onto me, sending me soaring. I cry out as pleasure takes hold of me, wrapping around me like a rope, twining itself over and over until I'm nothing but a mess of whimpering desire.

"Please, please, please." My begging falls from my lips as

my hands find Cassian's head, and my hips rock against him as I take my pleasure. His tongue darts inside me as he licks me like I've never before experienced. Right now, I feel like a virgin, experiencing sex for the first time, and my body sparks to life, causing arousal to drench Cassian's mouth.

"Just like I always imagined," he mumbles against me in a low gravelly tone that vibrates against my pussy. "Like a fucking drug." He trails his fingers up and down my core until two fingers dip into me, sending my hips sky high, and I earn myself another dirty laugh from the man who's playing me as if I were a musical instrument.

"Please, Cassian," I plead, meeting his heated stare that seems to scorch every inch of me. "Please."

"Tell me what you want, little liar," he coos before pressing soft kisses on my mound, which only empties my mind of any rational thought. I don't know what I need, to come, for him to be inside me, or something else. I'm not even sure what to ask for anymore, and I know he's enjoying my agony.

With a seductive smile curling his lips, he swats my pussy, causing me to cry out as pleasure wracks through me. Another slap comes seconds later, and another after that, sending me spiraling into an abyss of euphoria.

I've experienced agony before. But this pain is nothing

compared to anything else I've ever known. This is pleasurable pain, which I'll gladly take at the hands of Cassian Thorne.

Cassian

HER BODY IS NOTHING MORE THAN A PLIABLE MESS under me, exactly what I've wanted for so long. The sweetness of her arousal coats my tongue. I've never been so addicted to a woman's flavor before, and I know one taste of Kalyn will never be enough.

She lifts her head, locking those pretty eyes on me, and I can't help but smile at how glassy they are. Her pupils are dilated, her lips swollen and plump, and her cheeks are bright red.

"Please, Cassian," she begs once more, and I award her with another spank to her wet pussy, which earns me a whimper. Slowly, I slip two fingers into her tight heat. My taunting movements are enough to send her to the edge, but I don't curl my fingers to get her off; I ensure I keep her teetering, torturing her with an orgasm that's just out of reach.

"You'll come when I want you to," I inform her with a smile.

Her whimpers and moans are music to my ears. I've wanted nothing more than to make her beg, to hear her plead with me for more, so much more, and now that I have her here, I never want to let her go.

My fingers move steadily, in and out, sending her to the precipice, and allowing her to stay there. When her hips thrust upward, her need showing clearly on her expression, I can't help but stop.

"Cassian!" When she screams my name in frustration, I chuckle. "This is torture."

"Oh, I know it is, little liar," I taunt, circling her clit until her hips are once again undulating on the mattress. "And it's not going to stop until you beg for what you really want," I tell her. I alternate between teasing her hardened nub and dipping my fingers inside her. My cock weeps in my boxers for a taste, to slide into her, but that will come. Soon enough.

Pulling my fingers from Kalyn's pussy, I slide them into my mouth and lick her essence from my digits while she watches. Her cheeks darken, the soft hue of pink trailing down her chest.

"Ask for what you truly want," I announce as I push to my feet, causing her to whimper yet again. Once I'm standing, I unbutton the suit pants that are caked in her fiancé's blood before pushing them down and stepping out of them. Kalyn watches me, her eyes never wavering as my movements then tug at my socks. Once I'm standing before her in only my underwear, I halt.

She lifts her gaze, locking it on mine. "I want you to fuck me," she whispers as the embarrassment turns her tanned skin pink. "I want you inside me. I want to feel you; I need you to make me feel something. Anything other than this need for a high, for a smoke, or a line of coke."

Her admission is jarring.

"Even now, while you're here, naked and wet for me, you're thinking about drugs," I say, realizing just how much this shit has a hold on her. She doesn't respond because it wasn't a question. Instead of talking again, I push my boxers to the floor. A gasp of surprise falls from her lips when she takes in my hardness, and the glint of the silver bar pierced under the head.

"You're..."

"Come closer, little liar," I order, ignoring her observation. "It's time for that pretty little mouth to apologize." She doesn't sass me, which I almost expect her to do. Instead, she obeys easily, scooting closer. The scent of sex hangs in the air, her arousal engulfing my senses, and it takes all my restraint not to push her down and thrust into her.

My hands twine behind my back. My cock juts out toward her, right in her face. She's at the perfect height to take me between those plump lips. Gently, she grips me and elicits a hiss from me.

"You know what to do," I manage to grit out as pleasure courses through my veins, my blood hot, my cock dripping with precum as she tentatively darts that pretty tongue out and laps at my dick.

Every inch of my body, from my head right down to my toes, spark with need. I want to drive into her throat and listen to her gag, but I refrain. She wraps her lips around my shaft and slowly, ever so fucking slowly, sinks down toward my crotch. With every tight swallow of her throat, my hands fist behind me, my nails digging into my palms to keep from coming too soon.

Kalyn works me with her mouth. Sliding back, then dipping down, her throat tightens when the piercing hits deep, and the soft choking sounds have my erection throbbing along her tongue. Her hands grip my balls, holding them, massaging them, until I'm ready to empty my seed inside her.

My hands quickly tangle in her curls, and I tug her off my dick. "Enough." It's the first time I've ever stopped a woman from making me come, but with Kalyn, it's different. I want her, but I need to be inside her when I finally find my release.

I move around the bed to pull open the nightstand drawer and find a foil wrapper. Tearing it open with my teeth, I sheath myself before making my way back to my girl.

"Tonight, I'll use a condom, but this is the first and only time I'll do it, in the future, you'll take my dick raw." It's a promise, a vow. I can't imagine just how good she'll feel without the rubber on, but I will find out.

"I'm on the pill," she informs me, and thoughts of what that bastard did to her come rushing back. Before I have time to think about it, I'm on her, nestling myself between her perfect thighs. Her heat at my dick has me gritting my teeth.

I reach between us, fisting myself before I nudge her opening. Kalyn's back arches from the mattress as I slowly, gently sink inside her tightness. Her pussy pulses around me with every thrust, and by the time I'm fully seated, I don't know how long I'll last. She feels like heaven and hell, taking me to a euphoric place I'd never been before, and I never want to leave.

"Look at me," I command, my voice husky with desire. Kalyn's pretty eyes snap to mine, the warm chocolate melting into my cold teal. "You are *mine*." My words are annunciated with every thrust of my cock. Her walls pulse around me as if her body is trying to milk my release from me.

"I am." Her admission sends pride soaring through my chest. "I've always been yours," she tells me earnestly, and I know I can't hold back any longer. My hips move quicker, my body slamming her into the mattress. Kalyn tangles her arms around my neck, holding onto me as we move in sync.

"Fuck," I bite out when I feel her body tighten. She's so close. I reach down between us, my cock fucking into her deeply, and I circle her clit with my thumb, which only seems to make her body grip me in a vise.

My mouth latches onto the softness of her neck, the same spot I'd bit her before, and my teeth grazes the flesh. She shudders at the pain and pleasure I gift her, and I can't help but smile against her skin.

"Come for me, little liar. Give me all you've got." I suck on the spot while pinching the hardened nub, which sends her over. My words are a breathy whisper, but she responds with a cry of my name that echoes around us, hanging in the air above us.

Her cunt pulses, tightens, and her arousal drenches me as my own release skitters down my spine, and I thrust once, twice, and on the third and final drive, I grunt out my pleasure, emptying myself in the condom.

Kalyn

I HAVE NO CLUE HOW LONG WE LIE THERE, TANGLED LIMBS and sweaty skin. But when Cassian finally moves, I *feel* his absence. He pushes to his feet, and I watch in awe as he tugs the condom from his softening cock and disposes of it in the trash can. He turns to me, his eyes burning a hole right through me.

"Come, we'll take a shower." He holds out his hand to me, and I gratefully accept it. No words are spoken as we make our way into the bathroom while he turns on the shower and helps me into the space.

Once we're both under the spray, Cassian grabs the gel from earlier and fills his palm with the silky liquid. He grabs the sponge and lathers it up before tentatively soaping me up. The suds tingle over my shoulders, down my stomach, and he gently washes my thighs, my pussy, and down my calves.

I don't realize I'm crying until he rises to full height and cups my face with his hands. "Hey," he murmurs when he realizes I'm sobbing. "What's wrong? Did I hurt you?" The concern in his expression doesn't stop my blubbering; it only makes it worse.

Shaking my head, I offer a small smile. "No. I don't know. I just..." I breathe deeply, trying to find the words to tell him why I'm crying, even though I'm as confused as he is. "I haven't felt so cared for, not in a long time," I finally say. I wanted to use the word *loved*, but this is so new, I don't want to scare Cassian off. I'm not sure where we go from here; I don't at all expect him to profess his undying love, but deep down, my heart aches for it, and I can't *not* hold out hope.

Cassian presses his lips to mine in a soft, gentle kiss that has my stomach tumbling at the affection he's offering. When he pulls away, I keep my eyes on his as he regards me.

"You're mine now, Kalyn," he says. "There's no more running and hiding. And you're going to get healthy." It's a promise. One that makes my heart skip a few beats. "I may have gotten that bastard out of your life, but there's still secrets he hasn't confessed to, which we will find out. He didn't tell me why he targeted your father, or you for that matter."

"What did he say?" I ask as the water hits us both. There's something cleansing about this conversation, and I want to know everything Paulo said to Cassian because, even now, I can't deny I was stupid to stay. Weakness took hold of me, weakness at an addiction I didn't fight; instead, I gave in and wasted several years of my life.

"All he said was that he never planned to marry you. That he did knowingly hurt you so you could lose the baby," Cassian murmurs, his hold on my face fierce but affectionate. I want to turn away from shame, but he doesn't allow me to. "I made sure he paid for his words."

"Is that where all the blood came from?"

Cassian nods. "It is. I lost it, Kalyn. They had to drag me off him," he confesses quietly, his head shaking slowly as if he regrets allowing Paulo to get to him in that way.

"You did it for me," I remind him before tangling my hands around his neck to pull him closer. "Thank you." My lips brush along his, and that's when his hands drop to my ass. He grips me harshly, lifting me against his body, and soon, I'm pinned against the cool tiles.

"I did it for us," Cassian says. "If you think you're walking away from me after this, you're mistaken." The seriousness in his voice calms my worry. He's not joking, and my heart thuds wildly against my ribs.

"So, you really want me?"

A smirk curls his lips as he rolls his hips. The piercing at the tip of his cock brushes along my clit, sending heat and desire zipping through my veins. My head drops back against the tiles as Cassian's warm mouth captures the sensitive spot behind my ear, and he sucks it hard.

His teeth graze along the column until he bites down harder, marking me, and I can't stop my hips from moving to garner more friction from his cock that's nestled at my pussy.

"Dirty girl," Cassian growls, lifting his mouth to mine. "My fucking dirty little liar." His words do two distinct things to me—they cause every nerve ending in my body to spark to life, and they make me tremble violently before I feel him nudge my entrance. "We'll go to the doctor tomorrow because the next time this happens, it will most definitely be bare." There's a feral promise to his words, and it sends heat coursing through me. He pushes open the door and steps out, leaving me for a short moment as he retrieves a condom from the cabinet.

When he joins me again, I smile up at him and whisper, "Okay." I would do anything to have that connection with him. I watch as he bites down on the foil wrapper and tugs the condom free before sheathing himself. Even though I want to feel *him*, it's best for us to go to the doctor first.

"I want this." He jerks his hips, the notion clear of what he truly craves.

I lift my head to find his desire-filled stare on me. "Do it." Two words send him over the edge, and he doesn't ask again before thrusting deep inside me. A cry is wrenched from my throat, and I cry out his name so loudly, it echoes around us in the small glass enclosure.

It's fast. Quick. And filled with passion.

Cassian fucks me deep, hard, and with abandon as he bounces me on his thickness, which stretches me painfully. My body tightens around him, pleasure soaring, sending me to the edge, and it doesn't take me long to find my release. Seconds later, Cassian growls in my ear as he comes hard and loud, his mouth catching my lobe, and he bites down on the soft flesh, tearing another orgasm through me.

We stay under the water for a while longer before he lets me to my feet. Once more, he cleans me before washing himself. Once we're wrapped in towels, Cassian leads me to the bedroom.

"I want you to get some rest. I'll bring some food for you, and then we'll get some sleep. Tomorrow," he says, before turning to me, "we need to figure out the rest of Paulo's plan. It's not the end of him, not by a long shot, and I have a feeling he has more sinister reasons for wanting to play your fake fiancé."

I settle on the mattress, the high from earlier slowly easing with the talk of the man I stood beside for far too long. The pain and heartbreak I went through by his hand steals my breath, and the tears burn my eyes once more.

"We will get through this."

"You hated me at the party. When we stood there, you told me you'll make me pay for my lie. How did you change your mind so easily?" My voice is croaky. I lift my gaze to Cassian's, watching his expression change from affection to contemplative within a few seconds.

"For years, I hated what you did. I didn't hate you. I could never hate you," he tells me. "Deep down, you were always mine, and I knew it. When you left, I forced myself to be angry with you. I wanted to hate you so much, but even when I tried to, I couldn't. And knowing the pain you've already endured, knowing what you've been through, my punishments I'll bestow on you will be filled with pleasured pain."

His words slowly sink in. I have no way of ever thanking him for what he's done. Knowing that he's paying for my father's treatment, that he's trying to remove Paulo from my life, is overwhelming. I blink, and the tears fall.

"I don't know what to say," I tell him earnestly because I truly don't. For the first time in years, I'm utterly speechless, and Cassian smiles. "What?"

"There were so many times over the years I've wanted to kiss you, to touch you, to tell you how I felt, but I couldn't because I knew it wasn't our time." His voice is husky as he speaks. "But this is our time now, and nothing is going to stand in our way. I'll ensure you're safe. And when I get the details of Paulo's plans, I'll make sure he can never go through with them."

"My mother still works at one of his studios," I tell Cass; the thought of her being stuck with Paulo makes me shudder.

"I'll sort it out." He's on his feet and moving to the door in seconds, his phone in his hand. He glances over his shoulder at me, offers a wink, and then he's gone. I don't know what he's planning, and I'm not sure I want to know. The Thorne family has connections that lead to dangerous men, and it's never been a secret, but this time, I'll happily stay in the dark about what's happening.

I settle on the bed and snuggle into the sheets; the scent of Cassian's cologne still lingers, and for a long moment, I breathe him in. It feels as if I'm in a dream, as if I'm about to wake up from a weekend-long high and find this was all just a fantasy gone rogue.

The fear of losing Cassian when I've only just found him again makes my chest ache. Even though he's said he wants me, there's still a small niggling of doubt that settles in my mind as my lashes flutter and I fall asleep with thoughts of my future.

Cassian

WHEN I REACH MY OFFICE, THE SUN IS RISING ON another new day. One that confirms I've gotten lost in Kalyn and not realized there's work to be done. Even though I should be focused on getting Paulo out of her life, part of me just craves staying in bed and enjoying her body all day, every day.

I push open the door to find Finn sitting at my desk, his fingers flying across the keyboard of his laptop. He casts a quick glance at me before turning his attention back to the screen.

"What's going on?" I ask as I settle on the edge of my desk beside him. He's typing out an email with a list of orders, which he hits send on before he leans back in my chair.

"It turns out Paulo isn't the one running things," he informs me. "Harris spent some time with our *guest*, and he's confessed a few more truths that make more sense." Finn is focused when I lean closer to peer at the screen. There's no telling how much he's done throughout the night.

"Okay..." I draw the word out because I'm tense enough, and I don't need Finn fucking around with information on this bastard. "Have you slept?"

He shakes his head. "Listen to this. He's linked to an infamous ringleader of a drug trade that has moved its way from Cuba to LA over the past few years. This came to the forefront of his confession." Finn opens a browser of news articles before turning the laptop toward me. I scan the headlines, and my chest tightens with anxiety.

"Jesus." The word falls free before I have time to consider my response. Looks like the man who's in our basement is merely a lackey of a crime boss. "So, why did he target Kalyn? I mean, it doesn't look like her father has any links to this man."

"He doesn't." Finn's agreement has me pushing to my feet. If my brother doesn't tell me what's going on, I'm going to lift him by his neck and shake the information out of him. "The leader, whatever you want to call him, was running drugs, and Kalyn's little addiction got her caught up in his web when she was spotted in one of his nightclubs.

Hence, Paulo jumped at the chance to pull her in and get her hooked. The shit that Paulo was giving her was from his boss. This guy's MO is to get girls thoroughly hooked, bring them back time and again until they're lost to it. And then..." Finn's words trail off, and my stomach drops when he looks at me.

"This doesn't have anything to do with the drugs. Does it?" I don't need him to answer me because when he shakes his head, the realization that my ideas are correct has my blood boiling. "He's selling these girls."

Kalyn is young, beautiful, and loved by men, which means she'd be easy to get money for. That thought doesn't calm me.

"But can we take this bastard on? I mean... This isn't some jealous ex or abusive fiancé. This is a criminal organization."

"It is," Finn agrees. "I've spoken to Harris; we need to sit down with him and talk to him. He has his men who can help. Dad doesn't know anything yet. We have to do something. Girls are going missing every day. He sends his men out to lure the women with drugs, promises of diamond rings, and lavish weddings. Every house and club Paulo took Kalyn to—"

"Were this bastard's properties." I finish Finn's sentence as the pieces fall into place. "Fuck." My fist makes contact with the desk as anger surges through me at the thought of Kalyn almost being sold to some fucker who'd only break her further.

"We'll sort this out," Finn says, his gaze filled with conviction, and I wonder how my little brother turned into such an adult without me noticing. He's always been the kid who fucked up shit, and now he's the one telling me what our plans are. "Oh, and Damien is coming home in a couple of days. Hopefully, we can sort this out before our brother arrives."

"I doubt it will be over by then. Perhaps he can help." I stare at nothing in particular, my mind playing through all the scenarios. If we can get this crime boss in here, under the guise that we want to speak to him, perhaps get into the trade, we can take him down.

He nods. "I'm sure he'll happily step in if needed," he says, and I should know our brother will never let us face this shit alone. "Harris has the team in. They're being briefed on this *leader* we're going after."

"Manny Lopez?" I sneer his name with venom lacing every syllable as if it will kill him. I wish it would because I'd love to see the fucker take his last breath.

"He's pure filth from what I've read up on," Finn informs me when he pulls up an article, and I lean in to quickly scan some of it. By the time I get halfway through, my stomach churns with disgust.

"I've seen enough."

"How's your girl?" Finn asks, thankfully changing the

subject. "Any more shakes?"

"I didn't even notice when I left her now. I've been distracted," I tell my brother who offers me a knowing smirk.

"Oh, I'm sure you have." He chuckles. "I guess the years of waiting have paid off?" He laughs, and I'm tempted to punch him in the face.

"Shut it, pretty boy. Get your work done; I need the office."

"Go to your girl," Finn tells me, his tone turning serious. "She needs you. Harris and I have this. Damien will be here soon. He's taken the jet, so it won't be long until we're all together. We need to focus, and if you still have sweet pussy on the brain, we're not going to get through this."

Before I turn away, I slap him upside the head. "I told you to shut it. Don't talk about her like that."

"Hey, man, I'm joking. She's a nice girl. It's good to see you happy." His remark has me halting for a moment. "I can see it. I'm sure everyone can. There may have been years of issues between you two, baggage, but now that you have her, don't fucking let her go."

"When the fuck did you get so wise, kiddo?" I use the nickname Damien and I gave Finn when we were still children.

"Get the fuck out of here," he bites out with amused frustration, and I obey my brother. I head out of the office and down the hall to find Harris.

"Cassian," he greets. "I've got the men ready. This job won't take us long. We have far too much evidence, but we need the man in question before we can take him to the FBI."

"They've been looking for him?" I guess easily.

He nods. "For a few years. Now that we have an informant who's willing to talk, it will make things a lot easier. He's given us information on where Manny will be tomorrow night."

"Then we'll be ready," I tell him. I don't want to wait on this. The sooner we get it done, the sooner I get to spend time with my girl. She needs to know I love her, but I'm not going to tell her that just yet. When the time is right, when the moment is perfect, I'll finally admit my feelings for her.

"We will," Harris says, dragging me back to the present. "I'm going to let Finn know before I leave for the day."

"Thank you." I offer him a handshake before I head up to my bedroom. I wanted to bring Kalyn in here earlier, but I wanted to make sure she wanted it as much as I did. Now that we've taken the next step, she'll be sleeping beside me tonight.

I can't go to her just yet, though. I need some space to think. I spent the last five years wanting to make her pay for her little lie, but right now, I want to do more than that; I want to make sure she loves me like I love her.

When I told her I didn't hate her, it was the truth. Anger blinded me for a while, but hate was never in the equation.

Instead of feeling that dark emotion, I knew I loved her, even before she left. Our friendship had bloomed; it was so much more.

In my room, I settle at my desk, open my laptop and start doing some research. If Finn has Harris on this, I need to educate myself on what we're in for. The more I know, the better I can protect Kalyn, and help take this asshole down.

The sun is low in the sky by the time I look up from my computer. Another day gone, and yet, I still feel anxious having Kalyn here. Perhaps it's because I've locked her away like a prisoner. Maybe it's because I haven't told her everything about me.

I pull open the drawer to my cupboard, and I pull out the sleek velvet box. The birthday gift I had for Kalyn on her seventeenth birthday that I never got to give her sits nestled in the black material. I finger the pendant, and my mind flicks back to the moment I realized she was mine.

The sun is setting on another day in Thorne Haven, and the Havens are here with a few girls from school. My senior year, the last day of school. I should be drinking and enjoying myself, but I'm tense.

Finn slaps me on the shoulder when he steps up beside me. "Looks like the pool is going to be the place to be tonight." Since the water is heated, we always end up in the pool after a party. "Wowzer," Finn remarks, causing me to turn to see what's caught his attention.

When my gaze lands on the woman walking through the patio doors, my mouth falls open in shock. The speakers that surround the party area blare as Bebe Rexha sings about Sabotage, and the lyrics hit home when I look at Kalyn.

Kalyn makes a beeline for me. When she reaches me, my hand comes out instinctively as usual with her, and I pull her into the crook of my arm. Her white dress is short, hitting just under her ass, with a halter neckline that shows off her perfect tits.

Under the dress is a bright pink bikini that doesn't look like it's covering anything at all. If I say anything about it, she'll read too much into it. But then again, I'm feeling far too much seeing her in this outfit.

I've denied my feelings for her for a year. She's almost seventeen, and yet, I can't deny I want her. She's grown-up, more so than the other girls in our school.

"You're... I mean, you look nice." I somehow find words, but me stumbling over what I want to say to her is obvious.

"Thank you," she says with a smile that lights up the night. I've kept guys at school off her with threats, but when Brody Haven saunters up to her, offering her a look of interest, it's then that I step around her and keep her in my arms.

Kalyn's shocked gasp warms me as her head tips back, and those pretty eyes lock on mine. "What are you doing?"

"He was looking at you," I bite out, my teeth gritting in frustration because I can't keep her for myself. She's too young for me. But Brody is her age. They'd be perfect together.

"And?" Kalyn challenges, and I know what she wants. She's wanted me to admit my feelings for the past year, but I haven't. Instead, I've been the best friend. I've been there to listen to her cry at night after losing her grandmother. I've been there when she's been depressed about her family wanting to leave Thorne Haven. Each event that's happened in her life, I've been her rock.

But she doesn't realize just how much she's healed me. And she'll never know because if I told her just what she did for me the day we met, she might change her mind about me. There were times I felt more broken than a shattered vase hitting the expensive tiles of our home. But when Kalyn walked into my life, she did something. She showed me what true strength was. Even though she does stupid shit to deal with her agony, she hasn't taken the step I almost did.

And that's why I'll always be there for her. No matter what she needs, I'll be beside her. And if I can't do it as a partner, it will be as her best friend.

When I finally step away, the rest of the guys have joined us; two of them have girls hanging off their arms, which calms me somewhat. However, I don't miss the interest in their gazes as they look at my girl.

"Hey, girl," Brody greets, offering a hand instead of trying to hug her. She shakes his hand, a smile on her lips, but it doesn't reach her eyes. Once again, I've sabotaged the chance to tell her how I feel.

Fireworks explode and light up the sky from where the school is located. We should be there, but a private party was more appealing than spending the night with the rest of the students.

"That's amazing!" Kalyn's voice is filled with awe when a golden star, the size of the sun, fills the sky. It lights up her face, and I want so much to tell her how amazing she is, but I don't. Instead, I smile and turn my attention to the colorful display.

She is my star. My north star. Offering me direction when I was most lost. She's the reason I am still here today. But that's far too much information to tell her tonight. So, I grab a beer, hand her one, and tug her down to the pool to join the rest of our friends.

One day I'll tell her.

One day when I'm stronger.

Kalyn

I**T'S DARK. S**O FUCKING DARK **I** CAN'T EVEN SEE MY HAND IN *front of my face. The pain that lances through every inch of me steals my breath. There have been times in my life where I've had a stomach ache, or hurt myself, but this is excruciating.*

The pain radiates through me, twisting in my belly, but as I roll over, the agony in my back and pelvis seem to steal my breath. Something is wrong.

My eyes snap open, and I try to move from the bed; my legs feel like jelly as I wobble to the bathroom. My body is heavy, and I struggle to hold myself up. My steps are weak, and my knees are ready to give out. I feel as if I'm about to tumble over. When I glance down in the harsh light of the bathroom, I see it—blood.

"No." The word is merely a breath on my lips when the realization hits me hard. "Paulo!" I cry out as my head spins, and I drop to my knees. I hear him pad into the bathroom, but he doesn't rush to me. The urge to cry, to scream, to puke overtakes me, and I know it's whatever he gave me earlier. "Please," I plead, meeting those malevolent eyes, but he only stares at me with sick satisfaction as if he wanted this to happen. His unwillingness to help, to do something, cements my thoughts about what kind of man he truly is. Not that I didn't know it before, but right now, I know I'm engaged to a monster.

He folds his arms across his chest and leans on the door frame while I crawl to the shower. Once inside, I weakly tug at my clothes and find myself bleeding more than I was earlier. The stabbing pain in my stomach feels as if he's taken a knife, and he's carving me open. And he may as well be the one to do it because he hasn't wanted this. Paulo's made it clear he wasn't with me to start a happy family. I was nothing more than a distraction.

"Please," I cry again, but he doesn't move. My hands are on my stomach, even though it's not big, not swollen with life, I can feel myself breaking down. I thought I was strong, like I could do this for my father, be with the man before me. But as I sit there on the cold tiles of our shower, I know I'll never come back from this. I can't. My lungs struggle to pull in breaths, and as I watch Paulo glare down at me, I finally shatter. It's been years since I allowed myself to succumb to heartbreak, but this is my final straw.

I can't go on.

I'm no longer alive.

I'm a shell.

I shut my eyes, my head leaning against the cool tiles, but nothing eases the pure, raw pain that shoots through every part of me.

"I hate you! You bastard!" My voice is hoarse, scraping my throat with every word. "Fuck you! You did this to me!"

He smiles. "But you can never leave, or your precious daddy will die." Satisfaction is painted across his features.

Rage has me seeing red, and if I could pull myself up, I would go to him and hit him, throw something at him. But he knows I can't. I'm not capable of it right now. "I wish you would die! You heartless fucking bastard!"

My heart cracks in two.

I did this.

But I didn't.

It was him.

All fucking him.

When Cassian pushes open the door to the bedroom, the sun is gone, and I'm curled on the bed, my body shaking, and my mind awash with images of me dying here, on this bed.

The moment his gaze lands on me, he's at my side. "Fuck. I shouldn't have left you alone." The guilt in his tone makes me want to cry, but I'm too cold to even voice what's happening, what I'm feeling. I want to appease him. This isn't his fault. I did it. All those years, I kept chasing the high, the nothingness that took over when I lost myself in my addiction.

Yes, I welcomed it, but later, I realized I only wanted that high; that numbing sensation was because I thought Cassian didn't love me as much as I did him. At the time, I was hungry for his words, for his affection, and my empty heart devoured every fucking word without question.

"I'm okay."

"No, you're fucking not." He lifts me in his arms, and the shaking subsides slightly, but my hands are trembling as my body aches for a high. Just one little taste of something. "Fuck, I should never have left you."

His body cradles me as if I were a fragile doll that's about to shatter if he were to walk away, and for a moment, I think I might. Tears burn their way from my lashes down my cheeks, and my chest aches. My heart thuds against my ribs, the pain stealing my breath.

"Cass," I murmur, my hands gripping his shirt in an attempt to stop shaking. I'm not sure if it will work, but just having him close calms my mind.

"You're strong," he tells me, honesty dancing in his eyes and emotion cracking in his tone. "You'll get through this, and when you do, we're going to run away together and explore the world." The promise in his words settles my heart, and my stomach turns with anxiety as I picture him having to deal with me like this for the rest of our lives.

"I-I can't do this," I mumble, pushing him away, anger surging through me suddenly. My emotions are in turmoil with every moment that passes. This is why I never stopped. Each time I felt the withdrawals hitting me, I would just inhale a few lines to keep my sanity. It was the only way I could ever feel normal, feel steady.

But this isn't normal.

"What exactly can't you do?" Cassian questions, his voice low and gravelly, danger igniting every word. He doesn't move away from me though, he's still inches from me even though I tried to push him away.

"I'm a mess," I cry, sobs wracking my body, and his arms only tighten their hold on me as if he's trying to ground me. "I can't ask you to do this."

"You're not asking me to do shit, little liar," he confirms with his eyes locked on mine, confidence drenching his words. "You saved my life; I'm saving yours."

His confession hangs between us, my brows furrow in confusion. "What?" The word is a raspy whisper, but Cassian hears me. He's always heard me, even when I couldn't hear myself.

"A long time ago," he says, but when he doesn't continue, I reach for his face. The day-old stubble on his jaw makes my fingers tingle, and I trail them over his skin just to feel connected to him. "When we first met at the lake," he tells me before dropping his gaze to the floor.

"The night we met," I recall easily. It's a moment I'll never forget. No matter what we go through, no matter how much I've inhaled, swallowed, or smoked, I've never allowed myself to forget the moment my world changed. The moment Cassian sauntered into it.

And when he did, he was my salvation.

And I wouldn't have it any other way.

"Are you going to tell me?" I ask, still trailing my fingers over his angular jaw. The teal eyes I've come to find solace in find mine once more; the pain I find in those orbs steals my thoughts and claims my breath. "Cass?"

"I went to the lake to say goodbye. It was my way of letting go of life, happiness, and love. I didn't want to be like my brothers, or my father. I spent my life in control, and the ice that ran through my veins had taken hold of me. They all seemed so far removed from me at the time; I was alone. At least, I felt alone."

"But that makes no sense. They've always loved you. Your life has been—"

"I lost my mother when I was young. Finn doesn't really remember her, but I do. I did. With each year that passes, images of her in my mind fade. And at the time, I wanted to go with her, be with her. I'm close to Dad, but he and I aren't as close as my mother and I were."

I've never heard Cassian sound so heartbroken before.

We've known each other for so long, and yet, this is the first time he's ever truly opened his heart to me. The realization of that makes my chest fill with more love than I've ever experienced for a man.

I've always loved Cassian. I know that for a fact. But right now, seeing him torn, seeing his brokenness changes things. He's always kept his control, especially around me. But now, he's letting me in, and the thought of why that is tangles in my thoughts, and when he looks at me again, I can't stop the tears from falling from my eyes.

"You took it hard," I say, as I watch the expression on his face turn from melancholy to agony in a second. Just like mine always did when I recalled memories of my grandmother. We were so close. I could tell her anything. And then, suddenly, she was gone.

"I did. I hated everything. The memories. Photos, ornaments, even paintings she bought, everything in the house would remind me she was no longer there. And then, my father said he met someone. Anger had taken hold of me, and I went to the lake." He falls silent for a short while before his confession steals my breath. "And then you were there," he says as the corners of his mouth tug slightly, and I want nothing more than for him to smile. But I can't expect that after what he's just confessed.

"But what did I do?" My query is a whisper, one that feathers over his lips, those perfectly formed lips that have stolen my soul with a single kiss.

He stares at me for such a long time, I'm not sure he's going to answer. But then he says, "You saved my life. You gave me a reason to live."

My heart catapults into my throat, choking me of breath, of life because everything turns blurry, and the need that had been coursing through my veins is gone for that long moment as his confession sinks into my mind.

Cassian cups my wet cheek, his thumb swiping gently over the tears that have been tracking their salty trail over my face since he walked in. He doesn't say anything more, but he doesn't need to.

No one has ever said something like that to me.

I've never given someone a reason to do anything but be angry with me, to hurt me. The thought of me saving Cassian's life does something strange to me. My focus turns solely to him, and I realize my addiction, no matter how strong, wavers when it comes to him.

Cassian lifts me, carrying me in his arms as he makes his way to the sound system and he flicks the switch. We're surrounded by the gentle sounds of Conor Maynard singing "You Broke Me First," and I wonder which one of us broke the other.

"I-I couldn't have known." I finally find words, but they make no sense. "I mean—"

"I could never tell you. If I did, it would've put too much

pressure on you," Cassian admits easily when he realizes I'm still confused at the life-changing confession.

"But that means you lived with the pressure of keeping me safe," I say then, realizing just how much he suffered. He wanted me, just as much as I wanted him, but he kept a hold of his control.

"I did what I had to." There's no anger in his words, no guilt, just an innocent admission. He kept me safe even when he was dying inside. Another sob wracks itself through me at the thought, and soon, I'm twining my arms around his neck, pulling him closer, and I cry into his shoulder. I allow my tears to fall, not only for myself, but for him.

The song changes, and when "Crestfallen" by the Smashing Pumpkins plays, I listen to the words as the tears continue to track paths down my cheeks. The room is filled with pain and sorrow, but it's also filled with love and affection.

When I lift my head from Cassian's shoulder, he's watching me intently. "I don't want you to feel like you need to shield me," I tell him. "I'm a big girl. Everything you're feeling, I need you to tell me. There are no secrets between us." I tip my chin, locking my gaze on his to ensure he understands I'm being serious.

He may have seen me as a young girl in the past. Someone too immature to handle the truth, but I'm no longer her. I'm all grown-up. Anything he has to hold onto, I can too. And I'm no longer going to be kept in the dark.

"Promise me, Cassian."

For a long moment, he just looks at me, and then, suddenly, he laughs. The sound is a beautiful melody that fills the room along with the music playing around us.

"You truly haven't changed," he says. "At least, your sass hasn't," he adds quickly when my mouth falls open to argue.

"Fine." I can't deny it. Me challenging him will never change, and that's something he needs to get used to because I'll spend my life giving him a run for his money.

"Tomorrow, I need you to stay here," he says suddenly as he walks us to the bed. Somehow, Cassian manages to scoot onto the mattress, his back leaning against the headboard. He hasn't let me go, and I have a feeling he won't, not for a while anyway.

"Why? What's happened?"

"We've found out what's really going on with Paulo. Turns out he's working for some cartel boss." His words are cold, controlled, and I recognize this Cassian from all those years ago. When he was ready to do something bad, he would always offer up the cold shoulder.

"Cartel?!" Shock is evident in my voice, and he nods. "No. You cannot take these people on. They'll hurt you."

"I have to." This time, when he looks at me, I realize it's not a choice. He's not choosing to go into the lion's den; he's driven to do it because he loves me. He may not have said it, but it's burning through his gaze into mine. My mouth opens, but I can't argue. "It's happening. The plans are in place, and when I get back, I'm taking you away."

"Cassian—"

He cups my cheeks, both hands holding my face steady. "I'll always come back for you." His words settle my nerves somewhat, but still, anxiety tingles through me, reminding me that even though he may promise to return, nothing in life is guaranteed.

I don't know what to say to him, so I don't say anything more. Instead, I nestle in his hold and close my eyes. My hands are still trembling. My stomach still whirls, and my mind is still dancing with thoughts. It's as if I'm about to dive into the rabbit hole if I were to close my eyes.

I want nothing more than to get lost in a high, but I have to fight it. The addiction may be strong, but I have to do this. My future depends on it. Not only with Cassian, but my life. The person I want to be is at war with the person I am.

"He did it on purpose," Cassian says, but I'm too weak to look at him. "Paulo fed you this shit because he needed you hooked. It's how their operation works." I don't know why Cassian is telling me this, but I allow him to speak. "He wanted to see you become a toy for some sick, rich bastard who would've purchased you and used you."

The venom in his tone is nothing short of violent, and it causes me to shudder. Not from the addiction but from disgust for what Cassian is telling me. For a long while, I suspected Paulo was doing something bad, but never did I think it was anything close to what Cassian just confessed.

"I don't... I don't want to know more." I close my eyes and allow Cassian's warmth to calm me. "I just need to know you'll be there, coming home afterward because I can't do this without you."

His hand trails over my back, rubbing small circles from the base of my spine to my neck and back again. Round and round until I'm close to falling asleep. My lashes feel heavy. I can't open my eyes anymore.

Cassian's lips find my forehead, and I feel the warmth of his kiss. It's a gentle, affectionate action, and I can't stop the smile that curls on my lips.

"I'll always be here for you."

His promise sends me to sleep.

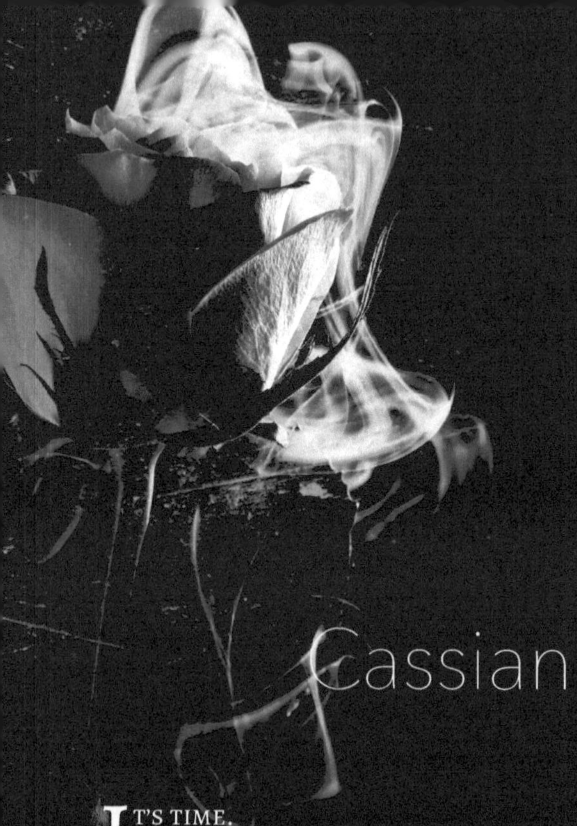

Cassian

IT'S TIME.

Even with the briefing I gave to Finn and Damien, along with Harris, I'm anxious. I've never been so scared of someone hurting Kalyn as I am right now. Paulo is here, beaten and bruised, but I don't give a shit. He'll be leaving with Manny soon.

The meeting I called was merely to negotiate Kalyn's release from Paulo's clutches. The ring she wore was nothing more than a ruse, so it won't take long to sort this out. But then again, a man like Manny Lopez isn't someone to be fucked with.

I know when I'm in too deep, and this time, the tide is

washing over me. I'm about to go under; the only thing keeping my head above water is the thought of keeping Kalyn safe.

"He's here." Those two words send my mind reeling with all the possibilities. I glance at Paulo, who's glaring at me. The hatred in his eyes is enough to confirm he'll never let this go. If he walks out of here today—alive and well—he'll come back to seek revenge.

My gaze trails to Harris, and I offer a small nod. A sign that confirms what I want done. If Paulo does walk out of here, he won't walk very far. The man I've known all my life doesn't move, but his eyes confirm he knows what I want. The expressive nature of someone's gaze is like a window; it shows you their true nature—what they're feeling, what they're thinking, and most of all, what they're about to do.

And as the patio doors slide open and three men darken the threshold, I pull in a deep breath, filling my lungs with air before I exhale, praying that it can calm me and keep me relaxed through this.

"Mr. Lopez," I say as I take in the older man. His dark hair has a smattering of silver, offering up a salt and pepper style. His face is creased with wrinkles, confirming his age. The dark eyes that hold far too much violence land on me.

He's dressed in a black suit, gray button-up, and matching tie. He doesn't greet me; he merely offers a nod. There's nothing about this man that confirms he won't kill at any moment. Even the men who appeared with him don't set me at ease.

I didn't expect it. But I thought he would be less... intimidating. He isn't. This is the first time I've come face-to-face with someone who runs a criminal organization. It's alarming.

All those movies you see as a kid, thinking that's how men in the mafia or cartels look, are exactly right. Old. Ugly. Fucking scary. I don't doubt Manny Lopez could take us all out with a look.

But when he glances around the room, I stare, taking in every motion, every flinch and blink, and I realize he's out of his depth. He's threatened because when he sees Paulo, he realizes we're not a couple of kids wanting a girl.

We mean fucking business.

And that's when I find my confidence rearing up, straightening my spine and tipping my head. I don't cower to the bastard at my door; I show him I'm a worthy fucking adversary, one who can easily take him down. One who isn't afraid to annihilate him.

The man in question steps forward, his two goons flanking him, but he doesn't scare me. Men like him live to intimidate, but I don't give a shit. This is my home, my territory. He takes me in, from head to toe, before a smirk curls his lips.

"So, this is the thorn in my side," he remarks, looking at me and chuckling. I don't move. Keeping my expression schooled, I arch a brow at him, but nothing more. "Paulo tells me you have an interest in one of his projects." His words rankle me, but still, I don't move, I don't respond.

"He has taken her," Paulo says, stepping forward, his gaze locked on the boss man. "I was getting some headway in when we returned to Thorne Haven, where she grew up, and then this bastard decided he's going to come between us."

"Oh, Paulo," Manny says, the smile still on his face. "Don't worry. A whore is just a whore." He's goading me. If I play into his plan, I'll fuck this up. Damien is on edge, watching, waiting. Finn stares at me; I can feel his gaze burning a hole through me.

"Mr. Lopez," I finally say as I unbutton my suit jacket, "I think we should sit, talk this through. As I explained to your man over there," I point at Paulo, "I'm not allowing her to leave this house, not with him anyway. If you wanted a girl, you should've chosen one that was more suited to your... *lifestyle*." I use the word loosely. Even though I'm ready to end this fucker, I have to bide my time.

The bastard is nothing more than a bully with too much money. He may run an empire, a criminal organization, but he's nothing to me. I'm not afraid of people like him, those who think that running the world involves fear.

It's a lie.

Running the world involves respect. And that is something that should be earned, not forced. Manny is the type of man who will instill fear with violence, and in that, he will convince himself people respect him.

They don't.

They're just scared.

He chuckles, moving around the living room as he takes in the furnishings, his gaze trailing over Harris, then Finn, and lastly, Damien, who's standing quite far out of reach of the rest of the men. His two goons that have flanked him are still in place, their hands at their front, and I know they're waiting on his order.

Paulo speaks next, "Manny, this girl isn't worth the time. The effort we've put in is nothing compared to what we could get if we just head out and find a few new girls."

"I'm intrigued with this town," Manny says before looking at me. "You own this town?" he asks while waving his hand in the air. The gesture makes me nervous, but I keep my features ice cold.

"Our ancestors built this town," I inform him easily. "Is that a problem?"

The one corner of his mouth quirks with a smile. "Not at

all, Mr. Thorne, not at all. I find it interesting that a girl like Kalyn would be at home here," he tells us.

I take a step toward him, noticing the goons flinch, their hands shifting to where I know they're hiding their weapons in shoulder holsters. "Why is that?"

"She's.... wild," he tells me as he settles into a chair before regarding me with a challenge in his dark eyes. He wants me to lose my cool. I have no doubt this man wants violence, and deep down, I want to give him that, but I know if I were to lose control, I'd end up losing Kalyn.

If something happened to me, to her, I would never forgive myself. So, instead of biting, I smile. "She's a lovely girl. One that belongs to me now," I inform him coolly, only to receive a snort of derision from Paulo. The thing is, he doesn't faze me, not when his boss is sitting inches from me. "I think it's time to make a deal," I say.

This piques Manny's interest. "Oh?" One of his thick dark eyebrows arches toward his hairline. "And what could you possibly have to make a deal with me, Mr. Thorne?"

"I have information about your business you'd rather keep private," I tell him. With every minute that passes, my confidence grows. Because the look on Manny's face when I say this confirms he's afraid. "And I have many contacts, ones that could ensure your import and export business ceases to exist."

It's not a lie. Thorne Industries has been working with several shipping companies, and a few calls have ensured I have the upper hand. I don't sit, I don't stoop to his level; instead, I lean on the back of the chair, my hands clasped in front of me as I lock my serious gaze on Manny Lopez.

"The girl for my silence," I throw out onto the table, with the hopes he'll see she's nothing to his organization. If I were to leak the evidence, the information I have, he'll be behind bars within seconds. I don't flinch when he pushes to his feet, anger clear on his face. But he doesn't strike me; he doesn't even pull a gun out. The goons that accompanied him don't move.

"Do you think I like coming here and making deals with children?" His sneer makes me want to smile. I want to laugh at him, but I don't. If I did, I'd ensure his anger would kill us all.

"Not at all, Mr. Lopez, but you can admit to yourself when you've been outsmarted, perhaps not by a child, but by a man." At my words, I push to full height, which makes me taller than him. Only by a head, but I am the alpha in this room. "Kalyn Narro is mine. She belongs to me. I don't allow my possessions to be stolen, taken, or even sold. I trust you can understand this since your wife was once a girl you sought out without purchase." My voice is controlled, my words confident, cool, which has Manny's face turning beet-red. I've called him out. He loves the woman he married, which confirms he cannot deny me my request.

One more moment.

Just one answer from him, and it will all be done.

I hold my breath.

But then, shit hits the fan.

Kalyn

Tension hangs heavily in the air. I should never have fought my way out of that goddamned room. Watching things unfold before me, I'm scared. I'm more afraid of something happening to Cassian than to me. The men circle him, but he stands his ground. Finn and another man stand off to the side.

Paulo looks worse for wear, and I can't imagine what they did to him. His face has clearly been punched one too many times. His eye is swollen, along with his lip, which looks cracked. Blood coats his face, and yet, in all the turmoil, there's a smirk curling his lips.

I didn't think I could ever hate someone. But looking at

the man I agreed to marry to ensure my family's safety, the emotion bubbles in my gut. When one of the men, dressed in a dark shirt with a black suit, pulls out a gun, a gasp tumbles from my lips unbidden, causing every pair of eyes in the room to turn to the cracked door.

"Kalyn," Cassian whispers, my name drenched in regret when he sees me. I shouldn't have left the room. When I found the door unlocked, I thought Cassian wanted me to explore. I didn't realize they were meeting right here, in Thorne Manor.

"Is this the little bitch that's caused all the trouble, Paulo?" The man with the gun questions, amusement clear in his tone as his eyes crinkle at the sides. I'm not sure who he is, I've never seen him before, but my guess would be this is the cartel leader that Cassian mentioned.

"Talk about her like that again, and I'll fucking kill you," Cassian bites out as rage drenches his threat, but he's not in any position to threaten. Even though he's not bound or hurt, there's no doubt the man in the suit is in charge here.

He chuckles, glancing over at Paulo before looking at Cassian. "We may be in your home, boy," the stranger says. "But I came here to get my man back. The whore can do whatever she wants; it seems anything with a dick will please her. Or do you get her high as well?"

Seconds later, all hell breaks loose as Cassian's fist makes a crunching noise when it meets the face of the man who's insulting me. Shots are fired, but I can't see if anyone has been hit with the bodies all moving in different directions. Suddenly, a pair of arms are wrapped around me, and I'm being dragged backward, a scream escaping my mouth.

"Shh, Kaly," I'm told as a hand slams over my mouth. The heat of whoever it is cocoons me, but the panic in my gut still twists with worry. I'm practically thrown into a room that I can only guess is a home office.

Spinning on my heel, I find the deep blue eyes of Damien Thorne glaring back at me. "What... What are you doing?"

"Saving your fucking life. What is it with women who can't stay in their rooms?" he grits out as he rushes from the room and pulls the door shut behind him. Seconds later, I hear a click. In the distance, there's crashing glass, more shots being fired, and shouts from a myriad of voices.

Looking around the room, I race to the set of glass doors that lead to the garden but find them locked without a key in sight. Frustration blooms in my stomach as I watch for something, anything to happen in my line of sight, but all I hear is the violence of men fighting for me.

Cassian should never have brought that man here. He should never have taken Paulo prisoner and tortured him. I should've never come back to Thorne Haven. I started all this, and I need to put a stop to it.

With my mind made up, I make my way to the desk, which takes up half the damn room. I pull open the drawers but find nothing of significance. Only paperwork. No keys. "Who doesn't keep spare fucking keys?" I bite out in frustration after slamming the next drawer shut.

A loud thud against the office door has me yelping in surprise, and I quickly move to hide under the heavy wooden top. Pulling the desk chair closer, I try to keep my fear from escaping in soft gasps when the door swings open, the hinges barely holding onto the heavy mahogany.

"Where the fuck is she?" the deep voice of the man who Cassian punched has the hairs on the back of my neck standing on end.

"Leave it, Manny." Paulo's voice is clear. "She's not a threat. She's nothing more than a junkie looking for a new man to offer up her fix." For the first time since I've met him, I've never been so happy at Paulo's insult because it just might mean this man will give up his search for me.

"Are you sure about that, Paulo? I mean, she's brought enough shit into your life." There's a dark threat in Manny's tone as he speaks to Paulo. I wish I could see them, but the desk is closed in the front, which means I'm safe, but I can't tell where they are in the room.

"Yes. She was nothing more than a distraction. We could've got some good money for her at the auction, but there are a million more girls out there, most of them virgins, and you know how much those assholes will pay for a pure beauty."

His words should hurt, but they don't. Not anymore. I'm done allowing him to add to the pain in my heart. I have to close my eyes and pray he can get through to his boss, or I'm a dead girl.

"Fine. Let's get out of here. Those boys aren't going to stay down for long with what we gave them. Get the men," Manny orders, and I hear footsteps retreat.

I'm about to move out of my hiding place when I hear a shuffle, which has me holding my breath once more. A few clicks, and then his voice comes loud and clear. "If you so much as utter a word to the police, I will come for you and your little boyfriend. I'm not scared of him."

I don't reply.

I can't.

Words fail me, but tears stream down my cheeks. I'm almost out of this. I'm almost free, but the price Cassian had to pay was steep. If he had never claimed me as his, this would never have happened.

But then again, Cassian Thorne is stubborn. If I tried to walk away, he would never have let me. Not when he had so many questions as to what I did that night, why I did it.

Footsteps ring in my ears as they near me. He stops inches from where I'm kneeling before he grips my ankle and tugs me toward him, lifting me to my feet. A scream is wrenched from my throat, but Paulo is fast.

I take him in then. Missing teeth, swollen eyes, and

a busted lip. They really did a number on him. A sinister smile curls his lips as he looks me over.

"You weren't even a good fuck," he tells me, but I know everything he says is meant to hurt me. "One last high for me," he says before I feel the pinch in my arm.

For a moment, he just watches me, but then he chuckles when my knees wobble and slowly give out. Paulo releases his hold on me, inadvertently dropping me to the floor.

"Oh, and by the way…" He stops a few feet away from me before he glances over his shoulder. "I'll make sure your little red-headed friend is nicely seen to. She seems like the type of girl I could actually marry." I know he's saying it to hurt me, but my heart is cold.

By the time I release a breath and lean back against the wooden surface of the desk, I'm shaking. Glancing over the top, I find the office empty. My heart leaps into my throat, and I move slowly to where Damien dragged me from, only to find Harris waking up from whatever they did to him. Damien rushes into the house from the back garden, his gaze immediately landing on Cassian slumped in a chair.

When I reach him, I find a needle sticking out of his neck, and my breath catches.

Shit.

Shit.

Shit.

Harris and Damien move quickly as they lift Cass.

"They're fucking gone," Finn grits as he re-enters the living room and realizes his brother is out cold. "What the fuck?"

"I ran out after Manny; it seems Paulo had something up his sleeve," Damien says, his eyes locked on Cass. I settle on the sofa beside him, noting his breathing is shallow but calm. I'm not sure what the hell Paulo gave him, but it must've been strong.

"I'll call Dr. Hoxton. He can come to the house to check Cass out," Finn says while pulling his cell phone from his pocket. "Perhaps easier than trying to explain what happened to someone at the hospital."

"Good idea," Damien affirms before settling into an armchair, but his blue gaze never leaves his brother. They're close, always have been. And it fills my chest with love watching them together.

My head is spinning from whatever Paulo injected into my veins, but my concern is with Cassian. I take his hand and settle in. I'm not sure how long he'll be out, or how long it will take the doctor to get here, but I'm not leaving his side.

And as I lean into him, my eyes flutter closed.

Cassian

The Past

THE END OF THE DAY HAS COME TOO SOON. BUT THEN I recall what's about to happen, and I'm thankful I'm ready to get out of here. School may be over for me, but Kalyn has another year left before heading off to college.

That thought doesn't sit well with me. I made a vow to myself to wait until her eighteenth birthday to tell her how I feel. If there's one thing I've learned from my parents, it's that once you make a promise, you don't fucking break it. And I don't intend on breaking mine.

Kalyn won't be able to handle what I want with her just yet.

She's still reeling from the loss of her gran, and if I were to drop a bomb on her now about emotions and relationships, it would only send her over the edge.

Even though she flirts, I know she's not ready. She's playing with fire, and if I were to give in, she'd only get burned. And the thought of her hurting makes me feel sick.

"Hey, Cass." Kalyn's voice comes from behind me before she launches onto my back like a goddamned spider monkey. I chuckle at her excitement and carry her to my car with people watching. The other students have noticed our friendship, some have commented on it, but I never admit to anything.

Yes, I do warn guys off her, but only because I know she's too fragile right now to get into physical and emotional shit with anyone, including me.

"What's got you so damn excited?" I let her down when we reach my Jeep before opening the door for her.

"Tonight," she tells me as if that should be answer enough. But when I arch my brow, she rolls her eyes at me. "We're doing the barbeque ribs for everyone. You promised."

"Shit." I forgot.

"Sometimes, I wonder how old you really are," Kalyn taunts me, tangling her fingers in my hair. Even though it's buzzed short, she still loves to tell me I have gray hair.

"Keep that pretty mouth shut, Kaly, or I'll cancel the ribs," I threaten, causing her mouth to pop open, and the O makes everything south of my belt buckle throb with need.

Jesus, I need to sort that out before tonight. She does things to me. Only a few more months, and she'll be eighteen. It will be okay. I know it will.

I drive her home while she changes the music a few hundred times as we make our way through the town and up to the Narro mansion. When I pull up, Kalyn sighs.

"What's up?"

"I don't know. There's a car here I don't recognize," she whispers, her focus on the Aston Martin parked behind her father's Bentley. "I don't like when they bring friends home. As long as it's not some shrink who's here to try to help me," she sneers, air quoting *help me* with disdain clear on her pretty face.

"Hey." I reach for her arm, catching her attention. "If they want you to get better, I think that's a good thing."

"I'm not sick, Cassian."

"I didn't mean like that," I tell her. "But talking to someone helps."

"Talking to *you* does," she throws back easily before pushing open the door. "I'll see you later." She gets out before I can say anything more as guilt niggles at me. I hate seeing her so sad. And even though I do listen to her when she wants to talk, I'm no professional.

But then again, who knows if some shrink can help.

Flicking on the radio, I head home with Ollie singing

"Fading Away" from the speakers. The gentle rap makes my chest tighten as I take in the lyrics. Everything he says is true, and for a long while after I've parked, I lean back in my seat and think about just how fucked-up life can be at times.

By the time I head into the kitchen, I grab a beer and swig down a few mouthfuls, and I realize I want something stronger. But I don't pour a stronger drink because the moment I get lost in alcohol, I won't be there for her. She needs me more than I need this. I finish my beer and head upstairs.

My phone buzzes when I walk into my room, and I pull the device from my pocket to find Kalyn's name flashing at me. I don't think twice before I answer.

"What's up, Kaly?"

A sob from the other side has my hackles rising. I'm ready to rush out to the car if she asks me to. I've always been ready to save her from whatever she's going through, and maybe that's been my mistake, but she saved me, so I can't turn my back on this girl.

And even if I thought I could, I know I wouldn't because, after all this time, she's burrowed herself in my heart. We're not just friends anymore; we're so much fucking more.

"My folks want us to move," she whispers as pain laces her words, which only seems to lance my chest. "They're even talking about leaving in a couple of weeks."

"What? No. You can't leave. You have school." My argument is pointless because her parents can have her move schools easily. "You can't." My voice falls to a whisper as I try to pull air into my lungs. It's a struggle. The thought of Kalyn not being in Thorne Haven, not seeing her every day, it hurts, it aches.

"I have no choice, Cass. They're convinced this will be good for the family," she tells me through sobs and hiccups. I picture her face, the tears tracking her cheeks, the way her eyes shimmer with emotion, and my heart thuds against my ribs.

"I-I..." Fuck, I don't know what to say to make it better. "You'll always be a part of this town," I finally whisper and then punch the mattress at the stupid comment. *Seriously, Cass?*

"I don't want to leave you," Kalyn tells me on a whimper that only twists my gut with agony at her sadness. "I've taken something to calm me down. I'll come to the party tonight."

"What did you take?" I ask, not caring if there's a party or not. "Kalyn, what the fuck did you take?"

"I think valium, it's something my shrink gave me a while ago," she whispers. "I'm on my way to your house now." I can hear her door clicking, and then a soft breeze takes hold of the speaker as she walks.

"I'll come get you. Don't walk," I say.

"It's okay; I'm coming." The line goes dead. I'm rushing out the door, down to my car with my keys out, ready to save her again. It doesn't take me long to drive down the street that links our homes to find her.

When she slips into the passenger seat, she smiles. "Thanks. Can we go to the lake?" Kalyn questions, looking at me as if I hung the moon in the sky.

"Sure." I turn around and head that way. Anything for her. Right now, the only thing that matters is for me to prove to this woman how much I care for her. When we reach the entrance of the woods, I exit the car and round the front to help her. Hand in hand, we walk through the trees, and when we reach the silver bed of water, we stop and settle on a boulder.

"It's one of my favorite places," Kalyn mumbles, but she doesn't look at me. "This is where I find…" She tips her head to the side, but she doesn't complete her sentence.

Curiosity wins out, and I ask, "What? What do you find?"

Kaly smiles. Then she pins me with a look that tells me the truth, but she only says, "Happiness."

"Oh?" I test, needing to know more. I want her to tell me what she's feeling. I ache to hear her admit her feelings. Those words that I imagine her whispering to me daily don't come. But I can't be too surprised.

"It's the place I met you," she finally whispers after long moments of silence, and my stomach flips. We sit in silence after that because I can't say anything more.

How do I tell her I love her when I can't be the man she deserves?

So, instead of admitting my emotions, I allow the sounds of the woods to swallow us in the darkness and the silver light of the moon to illuminate us. But with every glance I cast her way, I can't help but smile because she shines brighter than the sun.

My star.

My north star.

Kalyn

WHEN I OPEN MY EYES, MY VISION BLURS AS I ATTEMPT to focus on the room that I'm in. My hands tremble as I reach for the pillow beside me, pulling it closer, needing to inhale Cassian's scent. But even that doesn't calm me.

My stomach rolls at the image of Paulo and Cassian fighting. Memories slam into me, my chest tightening as anxiety churns in my gut. It's cold. So fucking cold. I'm shaking so hard my teeth chatter.

Tears sting my eyes when I realize this will always be my life. Every inch of my body feels as if I'm in a tub of ice water. I shut my eyes, praying for some form of solace. I need help. I do. It's been the first time I've admitted it, even if only to myself. But right now, the only thing I can think of is a quick fix, which is what I always wanted in the past. When I open my eyes, a thought springs to mind.

If I can get something. A drink. A painkiller. Anything.

It will allow me to get out of my head and forget about the mess I've made, the drama that has followed me to Thorne Haven. I brought more darkness to this town than I cared to admit. But now, it's here, and I can't run anymore.

Pushing to my feet, I rush for the bathroom and pull open the cabinet to find bottles of everything *but* pills. Frustration blooms in my stomach, twisting like a serpent ready to strike.

"What are you doing?" Finn's voice breaks through the noise in my mind, causing me to snap my gaze toward him. "Kaly?" Concern fills his tone as he steps toward me.

Surely he'll see I need it. "I... I need a painkiller," I tell him while trying to keep my voice level. "I-I... My head hurts."

He doesn't answer me. Instead, he wraps his arms around me, pulling me into a hug. I want to fight it, but he's so warm, just like Cassian.

"W-w-where's Cass?" I mumble into his shirt, my fingers tangling in the material as I try to pull him impossibly closer. He's always been like a brother to me, even though we're pretty much the same age, him only a year older. Someone who was there for me alongside Cass.

"He's still out of it. You need to see a doctor," he informs me before pulling away slightly to meet my watery gaze. He's blurry when I glance up at his face.

"I-I need... I just n-need..."

"A doctor." His response is no-nonsense, and I realize he isn't going to cave, no matter how much I beg. "That's the only thing you're getting." He scoops me up before I have time to protest, and soon, we're heading down the hallway. We pass by Damien, who gives us the once over.

"Put me down!" My voice is drowned out by Damien's chuckle. "It's not funny!" My tiny fists slam down on Finn's back, but I doubt he even flinches. My stomach rolls and I'm sure I'm about to puke on him.

"I'll be back in a few. Stay here with Cass; I'm taking her for a drive," Finn tells Damien, who offers me a worried look when he notices just how pale I am. I know I am. Usually, when I get like this, it's obvious in my face.

"Sure thing," the eldest Thorne says as we head out of the house. We reach the garage before Finn sets me down. The gate slides open to reveal Finn's black Tesla. I'm still shaking when I slide into the passenger seat. My energy is slowly diminishing, and I lean back into the soft leather.

"We'll be there soon," Finn assures me as he starts the silent engine, and I only feel a slight jerk as the car is in motion. My lashes flutter as the silent engine purrs under me. It's so quiet, I allow myself to relax into the soft leather seat.

"Kaly," Finn's voice wakes me from a dreamless sleep.

I snap my eyes open to find brown eyes peering at me. "Did I fall asleep? How long was I out?"

"Not long," he informs me. "We're here." I glance out the window to find an enormous house before us.

"Where is here?"

"Doctor Ulrich's house. He usually comes to the manor, but I thought you needed some fresh air." He exits the car, rounding the front before coming to help me. Finn holds my hand as he leads me up to the door that slowly inches open.

An older man stands on the threshold, a small smile on his face as he greets Finn. "You got here quickly."

"Kalyn needs some help, and if I didn't do something, my brother would lose his mind." Finn sounds so grown up, so much more mature than he usually is when he's joking around. My head spins when the doctor steps back, and the door opens wider.

Doctor Ulrich nods slowly as he gestures with his hand for us to enter, and then he asks Finn, "Is Cassian still unconscious? Is someone monitoring him?"

"Yes, Damien is with him at the moment," Finn informs the doctor before we're led inside and settle into a beautiful living room. Even sitting on the plush sofa, my legs don't stop shaking. Finn takes my left hand, sliding his fingers between my shaky ones, and grips it tightly.

"So, what can I do for you, young lady?"

I haven't ever had someone ask me that. No medical professional I've ever gone to has ever asked me what they could do for me. Instead, I was always ushered from their offices quickly with a prescription, which of course, only made my need worse.

"I..." I've never admitted it out loud. All these years, I have never once uttered the words. "I'm..." Shaking my head, I blink, and the tears I'd been holding onto fall, trickling down my cheeks. I glance at Finn, and he offers me a reassuring nod before I look at Doctor Ulrich and admit, "I have an addiction. Forced on drugs I didn't want, but I crave them now."

The older man stares at me for a short while before he slowly nods. "Thank you for your honesty," he says. "That's the first step. I won't lie to you and tell you this journey will be easy. It won't. But admitting it is most definitely the right way to go."

I nod. My fingers gripping Finn's so hard, I'm sure I'm stopping his blood flow. "I need help. It's taken me a long time to admit it. Even though I'm not alone in this, I feel like I need to say it out loud before I can start to heal."

"You're a strong woman to admit you have a problem.

Most who come to me struggle with that, but you seem to have come to terms with the fact that you have a problem."

He's right. It's the first small step. "Will you be able to help me or offer me some advice on where to go to do it?"

"Actually, Thorne Haven has a facility not far from the university," the doctor offers. "If you'd like to go there, I can definitely help you. You have a wonderful support system," he says, glancing at Finn, and I'm sure if Cass were here, he would most certainly be all for it. He's always wanted me healthy.

Even though I'm doing this for myself, I'm partly doing it for him as well. I want him to see me in a different light. One he's never seen me in. Cassian has been the hero all through our friendship, the white knight trying to save me from myself. I want him to finally see the strong woman who no longer needs a high to get through difficult times but can deal with challenges with a clear mind and a strong conviction.

It's not going to be easy, but I want this, not only to have him be proud of me but for me to be proud of myself too.

I make my decision and smile at the doctor. "I'd like that very much."

Cassian

THUMP.

Thump.

Thump.

"Jesus fucking Christ," I croak, rolling over to find softness beside me. Snapping my eyes open, I look into a pretty yet worried gaze that stops my heart for a split second. "What the fuck happened?"

"Paulo and Manny's men injected you with something," she tells me, her hand reaching for my face, gently cupping me as if I were fragile. "Finn and Damien got the doctor here to check on you. He said you were to rest. So, you have to stay in bed for a while. Your system needs to rid itself of the toxins."

"My fucking head is throbbing," I tell her.

"The doc said you can have a painkiller if you need it," my girl tells me. Kalyn moves to grab a glass of water with two aspirin and hands them to me. Gratefully, I swallow them down quickly while praying they take effect very fucking soon because this is not my idea of fun.

"I've spent my life hiding from this shit," I bite out before realizing what I've just said. "I didn't mean—"

Kalyn nods, then drops her gaze to the bed, focusing on the sheet instead of me. In a soft tone, she admits, "I know. I'm sorry. This is all my fault. If I never came back to Thorne Haven, you wouldn't be dealing with this."

"Don't you dare fucking apologize," I grit, pulling Kalyn until she's nestled in my hold. Her body is so tiny as she curls up on the mattress, her hands tangling in my shirt.

"There's something I need to tell you," she whispers, taking my hand in hers. "While you were out, I woke up; I was struggling."

My brows furrow in confusion. "Struggling?"

"The withdrawals hit me quite hard. Finn took me to see Doctor Ulrich, and he is going to help me. I'm going to go to a facility in town." Her words are merely a whisper, but there's a sparkle to her eyes which has my chest filling with pride.

"I'm so fucking proud of you," I tell her, cupping her face

with my free hand, my thumb swiping along her cheek. "You won't be alone. I'm going to be here for you every step of the way."

Kalyn nods then sighs. "I know, but there's something else. Before we talk about all of this, I think Genevieve needs your help," Kalyn confesses quietly, which makes my body tense. "Paulo said something about the redhead before he walked out of the office. She's the only person I know with red hair who lives in town." Her confession makes me want to make sure our friend is alive and well, but I can't move. It feels as if I'm being held down by a boulder, and the pain killers haven't kicked in yet.

Reaching for my phone that I spy on the nightstand, I open my messages and tap out a quick one to Harris. We need to get Gen back if it is indeed her that Paulo's sunk his claws into.

"I'll fix things," I tell Kalyn, but the way she's curling up smaller and smaller, I have a feeling she's not going to allow her guilt to ease. "This wasn't your fault," I tell her, but my girl won't allow herself to believe me until we find out what is going on. "He may have been lying. You told him you'd be going with Gen that night you met me. Which means he knows her. He knows about your friendship with her. Also, Gen isn't into guys from out of town, I think we all know this."

"I guess," Kalyn whispers as she lifts her pretty gaze to

meet mine. "It feels as if I've brought this all to Thorne Haven."

"You're as much a resident of this town as anyone else," I remind her. Once you've lived here, gone to school here, there's no walking away from this town. It has a way of burrowing itself inside your bones.

"I don't know," Kaly says. "Sometimes, my mind tells me I'm merely an outsider. Someone who should pack her bags and find a new home."

"You have a new home." My response is quick; there's no doubt, no argument in my tone. When her brows furrow in confusion, I say, "This is your home."

"Cassian, I can't. You know this thing between us is…" Her words taper off. I'm not sure what she wanted to say, but there's no way she's walking away from me, not again.

"If you think for one second, you're leaving again, that you're going to pack your shit and go to LA, you have another thing coming." I'm not taking no for an answer. "I've watched you leave once. I'm not prepared to do it again."

"But—"

"There is no but, because I'm not letting you go." I don't smile. I don't even offer a hint of a grin because it's not a lie. I'm not joking either. "We're going to make sure you heal from this addiction Paulo ensured you're a prisoner to. You will get better."

Kalyn has been mine for all the time I've known her, and I'm not letting her out of my sight.

Slowly, she nods. "I need help. I've needed help for so long but I never wanted to admit it." Her words hold strength, and when she glances at me, I see the conviction in those pretty eyes. "But I'm tired of being a slave to the high. To something that could kill me."

"You're not dying under my watch." My voice is rough with emotion. She's always brought out my feelings, tugged at the walls I built around my heart and made sure I recognized I was human. Alive and breathing. "If I have to, I'll lock you in my bedroom. I'll keep you chained to my bed," I promise, hoping to lighten the darkness that's taken hold of the room.

"So, you'd chain me to your bed, huh?" she quips; a slight hint of a smile curls her lips as she looks up at me, with adoration shimmering in her eyes. She's always looked at me that way—like I'm her hero.

"Yes, wrists and ankles, spread open, so when I'm hungry, I can feast; when I need a release, you'll be the only person who will give that to me." Her cheeks turn a soft shade of pink at my admission. "And the moment you finally submit to those feelings you have, then I'll unchain you."

"What if I've already submitted to them?"

Her question is interrupted by my phone. "Harris?" I answer quickly. How this man is standing, I have no idea.

"I found the girl; she's at work. Nothing seems off, but I'm going to take a closer look. Went around her house, and it seems she was there all night. She lives alone, but there were plates in the sink, wine glasses on the countertop. Nothing is amiss."

"Perhaps we need to talk to her, just to make sure. I'll meet you at the shop. Keep an eye on her." I hang up before he can say anything more. "Gen is at work. I'm meeting Harris to go talk to her."

Kalyn nods. "Can I come?"

"Oh, trust me, you'll come, but not right now. I need you safe. Stay here with Finn and Damien. They'll keep you safe until I get back to you." I press a kiss to her lips, and for a moment, I want nothing more than to deepen it, to claim her mouth properly, but I have to work.

"Come back soon," she tells me when I make my way out of my bedroom to find my brothers. When I step into the kitchen, Finn is leaning over the counter, watching the coffee machine drip into a mug. Damien is at the table, his computer out as he taps on the keyboard.

"How are you two dickheads feeling?"

"That bastard needs to die," Finn remarks when he turns to regard me. "Where are you going?"

"Harris and I are going to talk to Gen. Apparently, when Paulo left, he told Kalyn that he's found a new plaything, a redhead. I sent Harris to check it out. He went to her house, but it seems Gen was home last night, and she's at work now."

"What is he playing at?"

"I think he was trying to upset Kaly, but I need to make sure it was bullshit," I tell my brothers, who nod slowly in unison. I still feel like whatever they injected into my system has a grip on me, but I need to put that aside and focus on getting to Gen. "Keep an eye on Kaly; she's in my room."

"She better fucking stay there; she's as stubborn as Nesrin," Damien says as he rolls his eyes in frustration, but he doesn't look at me. Instead, his focus is on the screen. He's probably working on Thorne Industry documents, so I just offer him a slap on the shoulder when I pass by him.

"She will. See you later."

Pulling up outside the shop I know Genevieve works at, I shut off the engine and exit the vehicle. It doesn't take long to find Harris, and I head toward him.

"What's going on?"

"She's been working, nobody hanging around beside me," he informs me. "I called up our contact at the FBI; they're going to make a move on Manny. I gave them everything we found, even the confession from Paulo. He's waiting on a call from his team."

"So the bastards will possibly be arrested before we even leave here?" I ask, wondering if that will truly be the end of our fight with the goddamned cartel. Manny was a dick, but he didn't strike me as a leader of anything. Yes, he was all talk, showing off his guns, bringing in guys, and clearly getting the better of us in the fight, but there was something *off* about him.

"Let's hope so," Harris tells me before I head into the shop. The door causes the bell to tinkle at our entrance, and Gen glances up before offering a smile.

"Cass," she says, coming around the counter to hug me. It's a one-armed, friendly hug, and I'm thankful she's given up on trying to get into my bed. For a long while, Damien would take a bite of the red apple, but once Nesrin walked into his life, that all changed. Quickly.

I take her in, noting there are no scars, no bruises. "Are you okay?"

"Of course, why?" she asks, and I can't stop my assessment of her. Pupils aren't dilated; she looks alert as if she's had a fairly normal morning. Except she now has us in her shop.

"There's just been a threat hanging around Thorne Haven. He's targeting women," I tell her honestly. I would never be able to lie to Gen; she can smell bullshit a mile away.

"Honestly, I haven't seen shit go down in this town for a long time. Last night I was in bed by eight, and this morning, I was up late, racing to work. When I got in, I only had Hadley here, but there hasn't been anything out of the ordinary happening."

"You, in bed by eight?" I tease, a chuckle vibrating my chest. Gen has always been a party girl. She opened the shop a few years ago when her folks died, but other than that, she's always enjoyed her drink, her late nights, and company for the evening who she then discards as soon as the sun rises.

"Shockingly," she says with a smile. "If I see anything off, I'll give you a call, Cass. Thanks for checking up on me."

"No problem." I turn to walk out of the shop, but Gen calls to me, stopping me before I reach the door.

"How is Kalyn doing?"

I didn't think they were friends or even liked each other. Most girls in town don't get along with Gen. But her concern is welcome. "She's doing better. It's not easy for her to be here with her folks in LA."

"I meant..." Gen shakes her head. "How is she doing with the drugs?"

Sighing, I shrug. "One day at a time, I guess," I tell her. There's nothing more I can say. It's not something that you can just get over. Even though the pain killers I took earlier have done their job, it's not the same for Kaly. "But I'm with her, so she's not alone."

"She's lucky to have you, Cass."

"I know." I wink when she laughs out loud. "See you around." When I step out into the rain that's started pelting down, I find Harris on his phone. I gesture for him to slip into the passenger seat of my car to get out of the rain while I slide into the driver's side.

"Okay. That's good news. Thank you for letting me know," he says into the speaker, and I find relief washing through me. It must be Manny being locked up tight; that's good news because I can't imagine anything else fitting into that category right now.

I pull out my phone and tap out a message to Finn to let him know Gen is fine. They've been fairly close over the years, so I know he'll be worried. By the time I slip my phone back into my pocket, Harris has hung up his call.

"They got Manny at the pier," he tells me. "Looks like he's been docked down there for a few weeks. They've found a few girls stowed away."

"Do I want to know more about that?" I ask, my fingers curling around the steering wheel as anger takes hold of me.

"No."

"Paulo?"

"Also taken in. He's singing like a choir bird now that he's got the threat of real jail time. I doubt he'll be out any time soon, even if he does give the feds anything."

Nodding, I start the engine. "I'll see you tonight for a

debrief. Even though Manny is behind bars, I don't want to let down our guard. Also, can you get someone on Kalyn's folks in California?"

"I've already done that," he tells me. "Finn mentioned you'll need that done. I have to contact him to make sure we're good to go. All the clubs have been shut down, including the studio, which means her mom will be returning to Thorne Haven. The dad, we'll have to wait and see what happens with his treatment before we can make any decisions."

"Sounds good," I tell him before he exits the vehicle and leaves me alone to think on the past few hours. It feels like Kalyn and I haven't had time to really get reacquainted, but it's time I changed that.

Kalyn

BY THE TIME CASSIAN RETURNS, I'M OUT OF MY MIND with worry. But the moment he walks into the room, he doesn't speak; he makes a beeline for me. A predator about to devour its prey. I'm on the bed, so it's not difficult for him to pounce.

"Fuck, I've missed you," he growls as his mouth captures mine before I can ask what happened. He nestles himself between my thighs, his hardness pressing against me, sending heat coursing through my veins.

"W-what happened?" I mumble in between his assault on my lips.

"Manny and Paulo are behind bars," he informs me as if

he's talking about the weather. "Can we not talk about this right now?" he asks before I can ask anything more. His hands are on me, tugging at the tee I found earlier in his closet. I love wearing his clothes; it makes me feel closer to him.

"Cassian—"

"I always thought I would be your savior, and most of our lives together, I wasn't, but for the first time, I feel like the hero." He smiles at me, the brightness of his joy sinking into me, sending warmth coursing through my veins.

But his words have my brows creasing in confusion. "What are you talking about?"

He pulls away slowly, his expression turning serious, and I realize there's more to what he just said than I thought. He settles in and sighs—long and deep—before he locks those teal orbs on me.

"You saved me. I was so lost, so broken for such a long time. And you were the one who saved me first."

I remember him telling me that the night we met, he wanted to end his life, but I still don't see myself as his heroine. I'm merely a girl who fell for the boy who stole her heart.

"Let's call it even," I tease as I leap up and wrap my legs around him. "We saved each other." He smiles at my words, and his harsh grip on my ass confirms he needs me as much as I do him. "Cassian." His name is a whimper of need as his mouth captures one of my nipples and sucks on it until my hips undulate beneath him. His teeth graze along the hardened bud, tugging until I'm crying out in pleasure.

My panties are torn from my hips with a bite of pain that causes me to wince, and suddenly, two fingers are deep inside me. Cassian presses against *that* spot, sending sparks through every nerve in my body and causing my toes to curl and my eyes to roll back.

"Fuck," Cass growls against my skin as he trails his lips over to my other nipple and mimics the teasing that sends me soaring to the edge. My orgasm is just out of reach because the moment my body pulses around Cassian's fingers, he slows his movements. A growl vibrates through his chest, my core throbs with the need to come. Those teal eyes stare up at me from between my thighs.

A cry of pure agony rips from my lips when he pulls his fingers from me to bring them to my lips. He paints my arousal over them before crashing his mouth over mine and licking at me as if I were the most deliciously decadent dessert he's ever tasted.

"This is what I will spend my life ensuring you feel. Nothing will ever tear us apart," he promises before his cock presses against my entrance. The hardness slowly dipping into me. My arousal ensures his movements are easy, and he slips inside, sending me into an abyss of pure euphoria that shoots through every inch of me.

He doesn't move.

I snap my eyes open, meeting those gentle, affectionate eyes he's always looked at me with. For years, I spent nights fantasizing about him above me, his body cocooning me, and for a moment, it's almost dream-like.

"Hey," Cassian says, bringing me out of my thoughts and into the present. "You're mine." It's a promise I know he'll forever remind me of because once he's convinced himself of something, there's no stopping him or changing his mind. "I love you, Kalyn, more than anything in this world." His admission fills my heart with warmth and clogs my throat with emotion.

"I know because I love you too, Cassian." A smile dances on my lips when he slides out, then slams back in, stealing my breath, forcing a gasp of need to fall from my lips. He does it again, then again, and by the fourth time, my body is shaking.

"You're beautiful," he whispers against my lips. "So, fucking beautiful, it hurts to look at you." His words are a balm to my soul. I spent too long listening to a man who was happy to tell me how inadequate I was. Paulo convinced me I was worth nothing. Only when I was high did he ever want me.

"Cassian, please make me forget," I plead, my hands cupping his cheeks, holding him steady as he stares at me. There's no need for more words because our bodies move in sync. Cassian's hips move back before we connect once more. The way he stretches me, opens me for his cock, has my toes curling and my nails scraping down his back until I hear him hiss.

"Fuck, little liar," he growls, his lips brushing along mine as his tongue darts out and teases along the seam of my mouth. "I'm going to fill you up," he promises, causing my back to arch.

"Do it, please," I beg. It's like heaven. It's almost as if I'm high, but this time, it's a healthier drug than any I've taken before. This time, the high that tastes far too sweet is *love*.

Cassian fucks me then—hard and unrelenting.

My nails dig into his shoulders. His hot breath tickles my lips, and he steals them with a kiss that deepens with every drive of his hips. Our bodies are fluid, joined so closely, we're one person. The pleasure that courses through me is indescribable, and the moment Cassian bites down on my lower lip, tugging the flesh toward him, the sting of pain sends me soaring over the edge, and I cry out his name.

The mumbled sound is nothing more than a moan of happiness. He throbs, his hips slamming into me, and a rumble of feral pleasure vibrates against me when I feel

him pulse inside me; the warmth of his release causes me
to shatter once more, and I know we're forever bound.

Not only by pleasure.

But by love.

epilogue

Kalyn

Four months later

IT'S BEEN A LONG WHILE SINCE I'VE FELT TRUE HAPPINESS. And Cassian's given me that emotion.

He's gifted me with something I never thought I'd have again—a family.

But even though the sun is once again shining in my life, there is a dark cloud that seems to hang around. This time, it's my father. The table is set for eight—me, Cass, Finn, their dad and his wife, my mom, Damien and Nesrin.

A month ago, I said goodbye to Dad, and they were all there to hold me. To support me. And I'd never felt more times of heartache than I did that day. Even my mother was astounded at the affection we received.

I got to say goodbye, face-to-face when he came home to Thorne Haven. He went to sleep one night and didn't wake up. Usually, I would deal with the pain by getting high, but that's in the past.

I gaze at each face around the table, and I remind myself I am loved. It's not easy letting go of an addiction, even when you're happy and cared for. And every day is a battle, a moment where I could fall back into the same pattern, where I could choose a high instead of facing my demons. But so far, I've been strong.

Cassian's hand grips my thigh, and he offers a reassuring squeeze, catching my attention. His eyes burn through me, and I smile.

"Are you okay?" he whispers in my ear, and I nod.

Looking into the eyes that have forever saved me, I smile. "Yeah, I am." And it's the truth. I've been going to therapy and focusing on healing myself. When I told Doctor Ulrich I needed help, I meant it. Cassian's been beside me every step of the way. After spending a month in and out of the hospital, I've learned to focus my pain and talk it out rather than keeping it bottled in.

In the past, I wouldn't tell anyone how I was feeling, not even Cassian, but now, it's the first thing I do. We even have time set aside to talk every night, and Cass lets me get everything out.

He offers me an affectionate grin that has my heart filling with love. "He will always watch over you. I know it's hard, especially with Christmas and the holidays, but we're here," he tells me, his hand holding mine before he brings it to his lips and places a soft kiss on my knuckles.

"There's no doubt; I'm loved and surrounded by family," I tell him. "And I'm so much stronger now, I don't need..." I allow my words to taper off because I don't need to tell Cassian anything more; he knows. He always knows what's on my mind, sometimes even before I know it.

"I know," he whispers before he turns back to the table and we dig into the delicious meal. The rest of dinner is filled with laughs, chatter about gifts and opening them, and of course, the Thorne Haven party that will ring in the new year.

I didn't think I'd be so excited about the future.

There'd been a long time where I was lost, where I thought I needed a high to get through it. But even then, even when I was at my lowest, it was Cassian's support that got me through.

"I'd like to make a toast," Mr. Thorne says before pushing his chair back, he rises in one fluid motion. Lifting the flute of bubbly golden liquid, he smiles at each person. "This is a time for family. It's always been our wish to have everyone at one table. Long after the boys' mother died, I spent so much time alone; I didn't think a happy family was possible, but now, we've only grown, and I'm so proud of all three of my sons. Welcome to the family, Kalyn and her mom, Astrid." He offers a smile as everyone lifts their glasses in a cheer to us.

By the time Cassian and I head to bed, I'm exhausted from the long day. He slides under the covers beside me and pulls me closer, his arms wrapping around my waist, which immediately warms me.

"I have something for you," Cass whispers, which makes me laugh because I can feel his hardness pressing against my ass. "Not that, little liar." His growl sends a shiver down my spine.

"Then what do you have, handsome?" I question, rolling over in his arms to face him. His expression turns serious when he takes me in, and for a moment, panic twists in my gut.

"I've had this for years. I bought it for your birthday before you left, but that night, I never got to give it to you," he murmurs, his words making my chest ache when I remember that night.

Cassian grabs a box from the drawer beside the bed before handing it to me. Scooting up, I take the item, a sleek velvet box. I snap the lid and find a gold necklace resting on the cushion inside. There's a pendant hanging from the chainin the shape of a large, shimmering gold star. There's a diamond in the center, shining as I lift it against the dim light in the bedroom.

"This is… this is incredible, Cass." My voice is a whisper of awe. I've never seen anything like it, and when I turn it over, there's a small inscription—*For my North star. I love you*—with the date below it. My seventeenth birthday.

As I blink, tears fall easily down my cheeks. I fucked up so much when I lied. I should have been stronger that night. I should have listened to Cassian and stopped with the drugs and alcohol.

"Hey," he says, drawing my attention to him. "I love you," he whispers, causing my heart to leap into my throat at his admission.

"I love you too," I tell him earnestly. It's the most honest thing I've ever said. "I've loved you since I first saw you; I just didn't realize it then."

"Now you do?" he quips playfully as he takes the chain and laces it around my neck. Once the clasp is in place, I turn to press my lips to his in a gentle kiss.

"Now I do, and I'll never let you forget it." I smile, rolling him onto his back and straddling his hips. "I don't ever want to lose you," I murmur as I lean in and steal his lips.

Cassian deepens the kiss, his hands gripping my ass, squeezing until I whimper into his mouth. I don't think we'll get much sleep tonight, but I'd rather be losing precious minutes of sleep with Cassian than doing anything else.

Cassian

One year later

I'M PACING IN MY OFFICE WHEN THE DOOR OPENS, AND Finn saunters in, looking like he's just been told his puppy died. The corners of his mouth have dipped in a frown as he settles in one of the wingback chairs opposite my desk. I stop, look at him, and arch a brow in question.

"Did I ever mention how much I hate Dad?" he complains as he leans back in the chair, his hands behind his head as he looks up at the ceiling.

"What's happened now?" With Damien and I handling Thorne Industries, Finn has decided to leave the family business. When he told our father that he was no longer interested in being a *suit*, it didn't go down well, but finally, Dad agreed and gave Finn the option of doing his own thing.

"He's given me an ultimatum," Finn spits. "Even after he agreed I could do my own thing. He's gone back on his fucking word." I can't believe our father could do this, but if he has, there must be an explanation.

"I don't understand. He has never gone back on his word

when he's promised us something," I tell my brother, who nods in agreement. "What is he asking you to do?"

"Well, since you and Damien both have wives—"

My chest tightens. "Kalyn and I aren't even engaged yet."

"Well, you're practically married," Finn throws back in frustration while rolling his eyes. He's right; we live together, we're inseparable. "Dad wants me to... he wants me to marry some spoilt brat to ensure her father will sign a deal. Apparently, her father is some fucking bigshot capo that wants his daughter to have a ring on her finger before he signs Dad's contract."

"An arranged marriage?" My tone is incredulous. "But don't they tend to marry within the *familia*?" I ask, my hackles rising as I consider the ramifications of our family getting involved in something like this.

"Most times, yeah, but apparently this girl is special. If I don't agree, Dad loses one of the biggest contracts Thorne Industries has ever seen. This could make or break our family name."

"Jesus." Running my hand through my now growing hair, I lean into the chair and regard my youngest brother. He's always been a party animal, so for him to marry someone he's never met is a tall order. Perhaps our father expects him to calm down the partying and roguish behavior, but even so, I think it's unfair to ask Finn to give up his whole life to do this.

"Anyway, what's going on with you?" he asks, gesturing with his chin at the box on my desk.

"I'm going to ask Kalyn to marry me," I tell him; opening the box, I show him the ring.

Finn whistles as he takes it in. The star-shaped diamond shimmers on the gold band that is dainty for Kalyn's slender fingers. "That's a definite yes from her," he says, a smile on his face. "Congrats, brother."

"I don't want to think it's set in stone," I respond. "She could change her mind and decide I'm not for her."

"Like that will ever happen."

"Cass?" Kalyn's gentle voice comes from the door, causing me to jump to my feet. The box drops to the desk with a soft thunk as she pads barefoot toward us. "Is..." Her eyes are wide on the ring. I had plans on how I would do this, and now, now I can't do that because she's seen the goddamned ring.

"You've spoiled my surprise, little liar," I say.

"That's mine?" she asks, finally finding her voice.

Finn rises quickly. "I'll see you later; I think you two need a moment."

"Tell me what you decide," I tell my brother. He nods before walking out of my office. I pick up the box, pulling the ring from the cushion. Rounding my desk, I stand before Kalyn, then drop to one knee. "I wanted to do this in a more romantic setting, but since you're here, I better do it now."

"I'm sor—"

"Kalyn Narro, you're my life," I interrupt her. "You saved me, but you've also given me something to live for. You complete me in ways I didn't think were missing. And I want to spend my life showing you just how much you mean to me. Would you do me the honor of marrying me?"

Tears trickle down her cheeks, and for a moment, I expect her to say no, but then she nods and laughs. "Of course, I will." The ring fits perfectly on her finger, and I rise to full height to pull her into my arms.

"I love you, little star," I whisper the words in her ear before pressing a kiss to her forehead.

Kalyn looks up at me, her eyes shimmering with tears as she smiles. "I love you too, fiancé," she murmurs against my lips just before I steal them and dip my tongue into her warmth, tangling with hers. I deepen our connection; lifting her against me, I set her on the desk.

I pull away, locking my stare on hers. "You're a high so sweet I never want to come down from." Before she has time to respond, I kiss her again; this time, I inhale every moan and whimper. Time to show her just how much I love her.

My future wife.

My forever.

THE END!

need someone to listen?
You are not alone

If you've been through what Kalyn has and you're in need of help,
I've included a few links below that have information. Reach out to
someone.

United States

National TASC

United Kingdom

mind.org.uk

Australia

Health Direct

Canada

Addiction Center

This is one of the scariest books to put out there. After months of turmoil, I'm sitting here writing the acknowledgments to A High so Sweet. When I figured out Kalyn's past, it hurt so badly. Heartbreak. Pain. Loss. I hope that I've portrayed her as the strong woman I know her to be in my mind. And I hope that you've all fallen in love with Cassian just like I did when I saw how far he would go to prove his love to Kalyn.

I want to thank my amazing editor, Rebecca Barney (Rebecca's Fairest Reviews), who took this rough, unpolished draft and worked magic on it. I appreciate your insight, advice, and your expertise. It's always a pleasure working with you.

A thank you to Zainab from Heart Full of Reads for doing a BETA read of this as well. Your comments were truly helpful and it just added an extra layer of emotion to the story.

To my proofer, Brian (Illuminate Author Services), as always, a huge thank you for all your hard work on catching those final changes.

To my readers, the amazing ladies in my reader group, The Deviants, thank you for always being so incredible, and to my Captive Angels for pimping my ass out, you ladies ROCK!

To the author colleagues who read A High so Sweet, and helped share and promote it, thank you so freaking much! I love you ladies!

And to the bloggers and bookstagrammers who were so excited to meet these characters. I truly hope the book lived up to your expectations. Thank you for always taking time out of your busy lives to help support and promote me. Your love is humbling.

Mad love,

Dani xo

Dani is a USA Today Bestselling Author of dark and deviant romance with a seductive edge.

Originally from Cape Town, South Africa, she now lives in the UK with her better half who does all the cooking while she writes all the words. When she's not writing, she can be found binge-watching the latest TV series, or working on graphic design either for herself, or other indie authors.

She enjoys reading books about handsome villains and feisty heroines, mostly dark, always seductive, and sometimes depraved. She has a healthy addiction to tattoos, coffee, and ice cream.

www.danirene.com | info@danirene.com
Facebook Group | Newsletter | Spotify

other books
by Dani

Head over to my website to find all my titles!

https://danirene.com/books/

You can also find me on Kiss, Radish, WattPad